THE MENSTRUATING MALL

THE
MENSTRUATING
MALL

CARLTON
MELLICK III

Eraserhead Press
Portland, OR

ERASERHEAD PRESS
205 NE BRYANT
PORTLAND, OR 97211

WWW.ERASERHEADPRESS.COM

ISBN: 1-936383-64-0

Copyright © 2005, 2011 by Carlton Mellick III

Cover art copyright © 2011 by Ed Mironiuk
www.edmironiuk.com

Printed in the USA.

AUTHOR'S NOTE

So I'm not too worried about pollution, global warming, and the destruction of our environment, because if the world becomes uninhabitable one day we'll just build a giant mall in outer space where we can all live. I'm pretty sure that's the direction our society is heading in anyway. All we really want as a species is to move into a giant mall and never leave. Who needs trees, oceans, and skies when you have Orange Julius, Hot Topic, and Footaction USA?

This book was designed to be a message to the people. A message that stresses the urgency of constructing a giant mall in outer space. I swear somebody needs to get on that pretty quick, because our planet isn't getting any cleaner and Giant Outer Space Mall isn't going to build itself. So write your congressman and shit. Or else we're all fucked.

This book is also an homage to Luis Bunuel's "The Exterminating Angel," Agatha Christie's "And Then There Were None" (aka Ten Little Indians), and The Breakfast Club.

But really this book is just me making fun of myself. I'm a consumer whore, we're all a bunch of consumer whores. No matter how anti-corporate and punk rock we all think we are, we're still addicted to buying stupid crap.

You bought this book, didn't you?

I rest my case.

- Carlton Mellick III 6/2/2011 7:59 pm

HAMPSHIRE MALL

LEVEL ONE

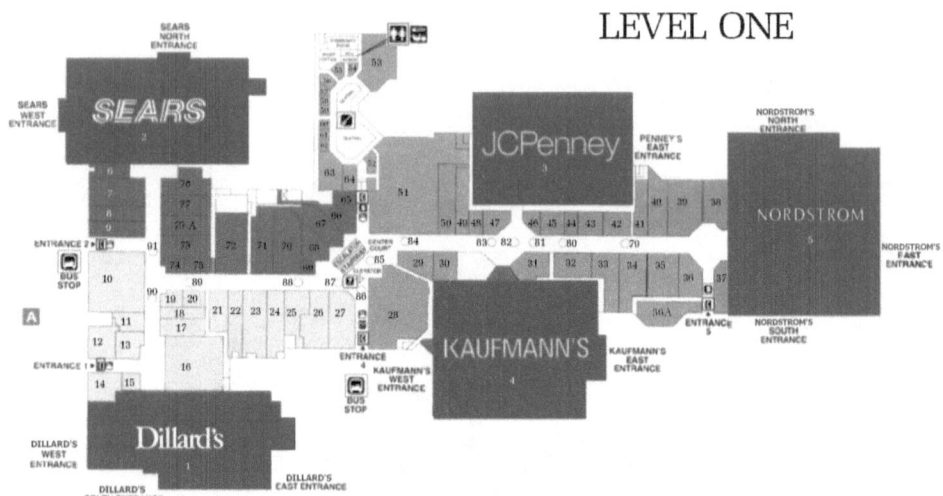

LEVEL TWO

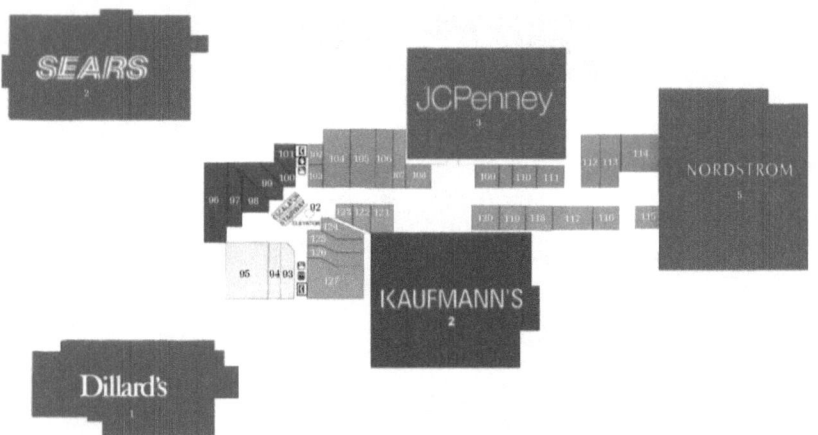

? CUSTOMER SERVICE CENTER	**FOODCOURT**
BUS STOP	**LOCKERS**
REST ROOMS	**MAILBOXES**
BABY CHANGING STATION	**TELEPHONES**
$ ATM	**TTY/TDD** (available in 2000)

MALL DIRECTORY

DEPARTMENT STORES

Dillard's 1
JC Penny 3
Kaufmann's 4
Nordstrom 5
Sears 2

ACCESSORIES

Extreme Sports Eyewear 79
Clare's Boutique 125
The Hat Club 17
Sunglass Hut 87
Rant 'n Rave 6
Ultimate Watch 89
Watch World 73

APPAREL

Allstarz 104
American Eagle Outfitters 41
Anchor Blue 121
Billabong Outlet, 120
Body Language 124
Burlington Coat Factory 16
Eddie Bauer 25
Forever 21 37
Frederick's of Hollywood 77
The Gap 31
Gap Kids 7
Guess? 75
Hipster Surfwear 105

Hot Topic 70
Lane Bryant 114
No Fear 45
Old Navy 39
OshKosh B'Gosh 30
Pacific Sunwear 34
Rampage 107
Rave 71
Torrid 26
Urban Planet 24
Victoria's Secret 108
Wrangler Wear 112

BOOKS, CARDS, & GIFTS

Christian Supply 36
Hallmark Cards & Gifts 9
Spencer Gifts 109
Things Remembered 78
Waldenbooks 65
Wicks n' Sticks 11

ELECTRONICS, VIDEO, & MUSIC

Game Stop 21
Game Wizard 116
Musicland 117
Radio Shack 27
Sam Goody 72
Smart Wireless 74
Suncoast Movie Picture Co. 35
T-Mobile 126
Verizon Wireless 85

ENTERTAINMENT

Children's Play Area 36A
Hampshire Cinemas 51
Virtual Action Arcade 53

FOOD & REFRESHMENTS

Chili's 28
Cinnabon 47
Everything's Pickled 14
Phil Donahue's Tortellini Ball 10
See's Candies 66
Some Fuckin' Hot Pretzel Place 92
Squiggy's House of Pudding 83
Starbucks 29
TCBY 46

FOOD COURT

Arby's 61
Butthole Barney's Bistro 63
Cajun & Grill 56
Chic-fil-a 58
Gyros Gyros 60
Jamba Juice 57
McDonald's 55
Orange Julius 52
Panda Express 64
Sarku Japan 62
Sbarro Pizzaria 59
Subway 54

HEALTH & BEAUTY

Bath & Body Works 68
Extreme Nails 86
Gapbody 123
Perfumania 22
Regis Salon 75A

JEWELRY

Piercing Pagoda 91
Extreme Sports Jewelry 80
J B Robinson Jewelers 44
Kay Jewelers 69
Zales 12
Ultra Diamond Outlet 103

SERVICES

Bank of America 93
Consumer Opinions 97
Corp. For National Services 96
Jenny Craig 101
Lenscrafters 127
Liberty Travel 94
Magic Photo 90
Pirate Surgery Clinic 95
Supercuts 98
UPS Store 102

SHOES

Baker's 99
FootAction USA   107
Foot Locker   48
Just For Feet   38
Kids Foot Locker   18
Lady Footlocker   113
Robert Wayne Footwear   122
Vans   111

SPECIALTY

Aqua Massage   82
As Seen On TV   49
The Disney Store   50
Excalibur Cutlery & Gifts   110
Extreme Beards   88
The Fairy Princess Store   19
Fuzziwigs   119
Hello Kitty   32
The Knife Shop   15
Leotard   68
T. Whittaker Tobacco   115
Vitamin World   100

SPORTING GOODS & APPAREL

All Flags and Sports   40
Big Barn's Sportshack   106
Champ's Sporting Goods   67
Extreme Sportswear   20
Finish Line   23
Just Sports   8
NordicTrack   33
Salvation Skates   118

TOYS, HOBBIES, & PETS

Extreme Hermit Crabs, 84
Hobby Bench, 13
K. B. Toys, 43
The Pet Pad, 42
Totally Yo-yo's, 81

CHAPTER ONE

There is no place greater on this round Earth than Hampshire Mall. I know, because the commercials on television tell me this. Their slogan says: "There's no place on Earth you'd rather be than Hampshire Mall."

And you know what? They are right.

They have another commercial with another slogan that says: "You'll never want to leave."

It is a very funny commercial where there's this woman who spends all day at the mall and then sleeps on a bed in the bed store and then wakes up and shops more. It makes me laugh every time. Most TV commercials make me laugh.

I'm on my way to the mall right now. In the parking lot, red-summer sun shining against the metal of cars into my eyes. A drop of sweat leaks down my back. I can't wait to get into the mall, into perfect cool.

After the mall, I will go back to the office to work more overtime. I work at least 60 hours a week, sometimes 70 if I'm lucky. If I have free time, I always try to use it to work overtime. Otherwise, I feel like my time is wasted. Money is very important. I want as much of it as I can get, and I don't mind giving up my weekend or my evenings to get more of it. The more money I have, the more I can spend at the mall.

I'm very excited to spend money at the mall right now. It is well-worth all of the overtime.

The mall is leaking some kind of rusty red liquid. It is trickling out of mossy pipes in the cement. I hope not to get any of it on my nice new shoes because these are very expensive shoes that shouldn't even be worn more than one day a year. I bought them at the mall's ultra fancy shoe store, and got the most spendy brand I could find. They must be the best shoes in the whole world, because they are the most expensive I've ever seen.

I can tell that the people hanging out at mall entrance 4 (my favorite entrance!) are extremely envious of these shoes. It's obvious because of the way they talk amongst themselves.

Inside the mall:

Cool air refreshes my body from the reddy outsides, turns the sweat into energy. Friendly echoing mall-voices embrace me. It is mid-Saturday which means everyone in the whole town is shopping here. Everyone knows this is the best time of the week to be at the mall, which is why I am always here every mid-Saturday. I once heard a person say they hate coming to the mall when it's crowded, but I don't know what they're talking about. Crowds make the mall come alive with action and sound. It makes you really feel like you are a part of something special and important.

First thing's first:

I want to go to the pet store to see the avocado kitties. They make me happy and sometimes I can put my hand through a hole in the glass to get a lick on my knuckle.

Kitties are cute.

My thinking-of-kitties smile fades as I pass by some scary-looking gangster teenagers who are strutting toward me with bent elbows and loose knees. They might be white, and probably only fifteen years old, but they still look really scary and I hope they don't want to rob me. I try not to look them in the eyes, but I can't help it. I look at one of them and he sees me looking at him. My heart skips a beat. His pointy eyebrows curl into anger and he grabs his balls and throws a gang sign at me. Then he struts away and his friends give him high-fives.

With the exception of that horrible run-in with the gang-bangers, my day is about perfect. I got to pet the avocado kitties, I ate some Chinese food in the food court, I bought dvds of my favorite Hollywood blockbusters at Suncoast, I got a few things at the As Seen on TV store, and I got five new work shirts!

It is time to go back to the office, but I'm having a very good day and think I want to keep shopping. I can stay here another hour and still work plenty of overtime later.

I pass by the Nordic Track store and see a familiar face:

Brock, one of the members of my work team.

I dislike Brock. He is the only one in my work team who never works overtime. Actually, he hardly works at all. He's always hitting on the girls and talking about sports with the other guys. Sports are great, everyone loves them, it's patriotic to love them, but work is a place for working not for sports-talking. At lunch, I always make sure to talk about sports with somebody. That is the right time to talk about sports and I sure do talk about them. I'm very excited about who wins the Super Bowl. But sports-talking should never happen during work hours.

Brock is testing out exercise equipment. He is flexing his muscles and looking at himself in the mirror. A customer service girl claps for his muscles.

I hope he gets fired. He ditched work on Friday. It's only halfway through the year, but he's already used up most of his sick time and vacation time. He only works overtime to make up for a day he's missed. What's wrong with him? That guy needs to grow up and get his priorities straight.

I wander through Dillard's and Sears, buy some new cologne, a new tie, and a new electric shaver. I want to look my very best for work.

Taking a rest on a bench near the fountain, a place swarming with elderly couples staggering in circles with wide open mouths, I dig through my bags to examine the new items I have purchased. I absorb their freshness, their energy. My fingers rub across the glorious cover of the new Titanic dvd starring Leonardo DiCaprio (one of my favorite actors next to Tom Hanks). I'm going to put this one on display with William Shakespeare's Romeo and Juliet on the shelf above my television at home.

Glancing at my watch: three hours have slipped away from me!

That's it. I need to get back to work right now. I do NOT want to waste my Saturday.

I get back to the southern entrance (entrance number 5!), looking carefully out the glass doors to make sure that the icky red fluid hasn't made a puddle in the middle of the walkway. I swear I don't want to get it on my shoes.

There's no puddle. I see some dribbles of the red gunk, but it is nowhere near the sidewalk. Thank God. My shoes are safe.

But . . . I still don't want to go out there. It's not the red fluid, I just want to stay at the mall for a little while longer.

Shopping has sucked me in once again!

I get a treat at Cinnabon and then go to Waldenbooks to see if there's anything new from Michael Crichton or John

Grisham. They are my two favorite authors. I have every book by them so far. I've only read a couple, but I own them all. I also own every movie that was adapted from their books.

A guy with a cowboy hat and tight blue jeans is blocking my view of the John Grisham section. He is reading a monster trucks magazine, even though the magazine rack is on the other side of the store, and he just ignores me when I try to squeeze around him.

He grunts and talks to himself with the side of his mouth. I decide not to ask him to move. John Grisham probably doesn't have a new book out anyway. I'm sure I would have heard about it on TV or at the grocery store if there was.

I really should be getting back to work, but I want to go see a movie now. It's the summer, so the hottest blockbusters are out. It's the perfect time to go to the movie theater.

I watch Terminator 3: Rise of the Machines. It is the best one in the series I think. It has the best special effects, which makes it better than the others. I don't think I like the ending though. The whole movie should have just been the girl robot fighting the Arnold robot. And the ending should have been like the ending of the second movie, where they change things so that the future of evil robots never happens. It's just more interesting that way.

When I leave the theater, I notice the mall is getting ready to close. The sun is down and many of the stores are locked up. I can't believe I missed out on all that overtime. I wish they'd let us work Saturday nights, but that's when the cleaning crew comes in. I keep pleading with them to let me work Saturday nights, even if the cleaning crew is there, but they don't listen to me. Well, I guess I can go watch Titanic again for the first time and try on some of my new work clothes.

I go back to the mall entrance and stare through the door. Other shoppers twist around me and go through the exit, hot night air blowing against my neck . . .

I can't move. My feet aren't going anywhere.

I look back at the mall shops. There's nothing open. Nothing to go to. So why don't I want to leave? Why do I want to stay here?

I feel like I'm in that commercial with the woman who doesn't want to go home. A snicker pops out of me when I think about sleeping on a display bed. That would be funny. I always wanted to be like the people in commercials.

But those stores are locked up. There's no way I can sleep on a display bed. I need to just go home.

Staring out of the doors . . .

"Time to go," I say to myself.

I hide in the public bathroom by the food court, lock myself into a stall and sit on the toilet seat, admiring the burrito-folding device I got at the As Seen on TV store.

All the sounds of the mall hush to a silence.

A couple hours pass.

A janitor enters the bathroom.

He opens the stalls one at a time and urinates into each toilet.

When he gets to my stall, the handicapped stall, he can't get the door open. He tugs on it, shakes it, and then makes a hmmmrph sound. Like he thinks something is wrong with the door. But he doesn't try to get in. Just gives up. He doesn't even bother looking under the door to see if someone is hiding here.

The janitor lights a cigarette and takes a few drags, then tosses it over the door into my stall. It lands on the floor by my toes. I don't move. He lights another cigarette and then tosses that one over the door. It lands on my lap and I brush it off into the toilet bowl. He lights another one and smokes most of it before tossing it into the stall next to me. It rolls under the divider toward my feet.

The janitor mops the floor for half a minute, then turns out the light and leaves. A dim light above the sink illuminates the room with a gray glow. The cigarettes by my new fancy shoes burn like two red eyes.

A couple more hours pass and the door opens again. No wait, not the door. Something else. A plate in the ceiling is being removed. I see legs drop out of the ceiling above me and balance on the top of my stall. It's a girl. Some kind of witchy girl with short tangled hair and dark makeup. Her lacy black dress rips as she climbs down into the stall next to mine.

She hasn't noticed me. She sits on the toilet and urinates, tapping her feet and humming some kind of tune. I don't make a noise, try not to even breathe. When she is done, she wipes and pulls up her underwear. Then climbs back up into the ceiling.

She doesn't flush. I want to go into that stall and flush the toilet for her, because not flushing is just gross. But I guess somebody might hear it and come investigating.

I don't know what I'd do if somebody caught me in here.

Sunday.

I wake up in the toilet and check my watch. The mall is about to open.

I leave the bathroom with an aching head, shopping bags

thrown over my shoulders. Stretch out my back in the food court and then journey to the south entrance.

Still can't leave.

What is going on? Why won't I leave?

I wander around the mall until the shops are open and then I buy some more things. CDs and movies. I eat at Chick-fil-A and then go watch the new Sandra Bullock movie at the theater. It is pretty good. All Sandra Bullock movies are pretty good.

I try to leave again. No luck. I eat Sbarro's and browse Sam Goody.

Brock is back at the mall. He's now at Champ's, trying on sports clothes and flexing his muscles in the mirror. He kisses his muscles. Then he pretends he has his muscled arm around a hot chick. With his other arm, he pretends to grab the imaginary woman's breast while flexing his muscles in a kind of pose. I make sure he doesn't see me.

I go to the Pet Pad to see the avocado kitties so they can cheer me up, but the kitties aren't there anymore. Somebody must have bought both of them.

For dinner, I go to Chili's and get the mushroom jack fajitas. Chili's makes the best Mexican food in the world. My shopping bags are sitting across from me like they are my date. I look at their logos as though I'm looking into a beautiful woman's eyes, and I smile. Shopping bags always make me smile.

The mall closes early today. I stand in front of the exit, trying to find my car out in the parking lot. It is too far away. An hour passes. I just can't leave.

The food court is empty except for one person, sitting at a table. It is one of the white gangster kids. The one who threw a gang sign at me yesterday.

He looks sick. He is eating stale food that he probably dug out of the trash can.

"What ya doin in my food court, richy?" he says, throwing a very complicated gang sign that makes him look like he is doing the chicken dance.

"Do you work here?" I ask him.

"I own da place, bitch," he says, pointing his fingers gun-shaped at me. "Get the fuck out before I cap yo ass, white boy!"

I speed-walk away from the teenager, hoping he doesn't shoot at me. I've heard about all the shootings at the mall.

I'm not sure why he called me "white boy" though. He's a blond-haired, blue-eyed Aryan. I might have red hair and freckles, but my dad was mostly Portuguese. That kid is more of a white boy than I am.

Outside of the food court, I look back and he's grabbing his balls and throwing more gang signs at me, muttering something about his gat.

Back in the bathroom, I get to sleep pretty easily. I dream of cigarettes hitting me in the head and a witchy girl taking a dump in the stall next to me.

I don't dream about work. My dreams are usually about work, but now my dreams are about the mall. Living inside of the mall.

CHAPTER TWO

Monday.

I need to get to work.

I get a mocha at Starbucks. Take a deep breath. Then try to leave.

At the exit, looking through the door. Can't move. Can't even touch the door anymore.

I look over to my right and jump as I see the white gangster kid at my side. But he isn't looking at me. He is gazing through the door, in some kind of trance.

"Don't you have school?" I ask him.

The kid's voice is soft. "It's summer, bitch. Don't talk to me."

"You can't leave either," I say.

"I can leave whenever I want, yo," he says. "I just don't want to."

He kind of throws a very simplistic half-assed gang sign and walks away, sadly.

I run into Brock at the entrance of FootAction USA. He's waiting for the store to open, admiring his reflection in the glass.

"Aren't you supposed to be at work," he says to me, looking at my reflection in the mirror.

A quick lie: "I needed to get a suit."

"You had all weekend to get a suit," he tells me.

I walk away, wandering aimlessly through the mall. My arms ache from carrying the bags around. I try shopping, but it's just not any fun right now. I've decided not to buy anything else because I don't want to carry more bags around. Not to mention I'm running out of money on my debit card. I should save it for food. God knows how long I'll be stuck here.

I try again. I need to get to the office. I'm already a couple hours late. This time I'm going to leave for sure. No matter what it takes. I'll just close my eyes and run through the door. It *has* to work.

At the south entrance: I can't get within arms-length of the door this time. My feet just won't move. I close my eyes, but my feet won't go. I try to drop my weight toward the door, hoping to fall through, but somehow gravity isn't working right. My body won't fall forward, just back.

I drop to the floor and crawl into a corner. My face squeezes into my knees and I begin to cry. There's nothing else I can do. I can't go to work. I can't go shopping. I can't pet the avocado kitties. So I just cry.

Almost an hour passes. A figure stands over me, looking down. I wipe the tears out of my eyes to see Brock. His beefy body flexes at me, with several bags of shopping under his arms.

I try to speak, but my voice cracks. I have to force the words out of me, "I-I c-can't . . . leave."

My hand wipes snot from my face. "Please . . . help me. Pick me up and throw me out of here if you have to. I don't know what's happening to me. I can't get out of the mall."

Setting down his bags, he holds out his hand and pulls me off of the floor.

He stares at me with an angry face. I bet he thinks I'm crazy.

But then, out of nowhere, a tear falls down his cheek.
And he says, "Neither can I."

We get some mochas at Starbucks and find a seat in the food
court. It's almost lunch time, so most of the tables are full.

"I've been here since Friday," Brock says. "I came here during my break but never went back to work. At first, I thought I
didn't want to go. I thought I could leave if I wanted to, but I
can't. I thought I was going crazy."

"I thought I was crazy," I tell him.

"I've tried everything," he says. "Last night I didn't even
hide when the mall closed. I wanted a security guard to physically throw me out. But there weren't any security guards. I
slept on a bench in plain view, but nobody was around to do
anything."

"There's got to be something we can do," I say.

His face is red and puffy at me.

"Excuse me." A woman taps me on the shoulder. She is covered
in tears. Her voice is jittery.

We look up at her, a mid-thirties blonde woman with twice
as many bags as Brock and I.

"Did you say you're trapped in the mall?" she asks. "You
can't get out?"

She's one of us.

"I've been stuck here too," she sits down next to me, wiping
her tears away. "I've been trying to leave but I can't. I dropped
my kids off at school last week and came to the mall like any
other day, but by the time school was out I couldn't leave. I

never picked up my kids. I never made dinner for my husband . . ."

"Something's terribly wrong here," says a cowboy with a monster truck magazine.

He sits down at our table and speaks through the side of his mouth, "I've been stuck here, too."

We're not sure if the two are together or if they just happened to both overhear us at once.

"Christ," Brock says, flexing a fist. "What the hell is going on here?"

Four of us now. I'm beginning to feel a little better. Just a little more comfortable with the situation.

"At least we're not alone in this," I say.

The two strangers introduce themselves. The woman's name is Wyoming. And the cowboy's name is Aaron.

"I wonder if there's anymore people like us," Brock says.

"I think there's at least one or two more," I say.

"I'm never going to see my babies again," cries Wyoming.

The cowboy tries to comfort her, but she is beginning to get hysterical.

"I'm such a horrible mother!" she says. "I haven't even called them! They probably think I'm—"

A silence hits us.

"What the . . . fuck?" Brock says. "Where did everybody go?"

I look away from Wyoming and examine the area around us. All the tables in the food court are empty. Everyone's gone. Disappeared.

"I didn't see anybody get up and walk away," I say.

Even the mall employees are missing. Food is cooking behind the counter at Cajun & Grill, but nobody is monitoring it. Their post has been abandoned. The entire food court is abandoned, at the most crowded time of the day.

The silence is interrupted by an echoing boom as doors to the arcade burst open.

The white gangster kid is race-strutting to us.

"What's going on, yo?" he calls.

"Everyone disappeared," I say.

He says, "Why'd they bail, yo?"

Brock doesn't say a word to the kid, charging out of the food court and looking around. There isn't anybody anywhere. The place is completely empty of life. We run to the south entrance, the white gangster kid follows. This time, we can't get within ten feet of the entrance. We stare outside, through the doors.

Everyone is outside. Hundreds of people crowding the parking lot, looking inside at us.

"What're they doing?" Wyoming cries. "Why are they just looking at us like that?"

Their faces are lifeless, blank, staring at us with open mouths. They are motionless, like paintings.

"Something is very, very wrong," Brock says.

We leave our bags in the food court, and go looking for more people in the mall, calling out for help.

"Let's split up," Brock says. "What's your name, kid?" he asks the white gangster.

"C-dogg, wes'side," he says.

"Your real name, dipshit," Brock says.

"That IS my real name, bitch."

"Fuck it," Brock says, he turns to me. "You take this kid and Aaron. I'll go with Wyoming."

"Fuck that," C-dogg says. "I ain't goin with no racist redneck and a white richy."

"Aren't you white?" Brock asks.

"My dad was part black, yo," he says. "I'm at least 10% black."

Brock brushes him off and walks away, Wyoming and Aaron follow after. Leaving me with the white gangster kid.

"Let's go," I tell him.

"Shit, bitch," the kid says, strutting behind me and bobbing his head back and forth with his steps.

Pacing through the empty mall, calling out for anyone who will answer. The kid doesn't help me call to people, just strutting behind me with his hat on sideways, mumble-rapping about 40s and blunts and bitches to himself.

"Is anyone there?" My voice echoes.

No response.

The emptiness is unnerving, haunting. The mall is no longer a happy, lively place. Its magic has become black. Near the end of the mall, we find someone sitting on a bench by the fountain. An old man.

"Didn't you hear us?" I ask the old man.

He is smiling at the fountain, ignoring me.

I stand in front of him. One of his eyes is fake, a glass eye pointed in the wrong direction. His smile is uncomfortably large, big rotten teeth, large furry eyebrows. He's just staring at the water.

"What's up with him?" C-dogg asks.

The old man giggles like a little girl at us.

He has several shopping bags next to him, all from the Fairytale Princess store.

"My wife died here a few years ago," the old man says. "Right where I'm sitting. She was laughing when she died. I can see her in the water sometimes. Just laughing."

"Is anyone else around here?" I ask him.

"I need to buy some mermaid-flavored toothpaste," he says.

The white kid shrugs at me.

The old man wiggles in his seat. "I want a pillow made out of ice cream."

The mall intercom beeps on. Brock's voice: "Everyone in the mall, please meet in the food court. If you can here me, you're not alone."

He repeats this and then hangs up.

"We need to go to the food court," I tell the old man.

He is back in his own world again. Staring at the fountain with evil eyebrows, BIG smile on his face.

"Let's just leave him, yo," the kid says.

"Help me out," I say, pulling the old man to his feet.

We practically have to drag him through the mall. His face still locked in a crazed expression, legs like stiff boards.

In the food court: two new faces. An obese middle-aged woman and a black guy—a little younger than me, probably mid-twenties but dressed like a teenaged punk rocker. Blue dreadlocks, broken glasses, piercings, a skateboard.

The obese woman is blathering about something, but nobody is listening to her. Every other sentence has the word "Jesus" in it. The black guy seems calm, unbothered yet interested by the situation.

"We must have been brain-washed somehow," the black guy says. "Like we're guinea pigs for some kind of subliminal advertising experiment."

The white gangster gets excited to see a real live black person here. He says, "Wassup, brutha," and sits down next to him like he's his old childhood friend. The black skater just ignores him.

Two young girls arrive after us. They are not together but arrive at the same time.

"Daaaammnn!" C-dogg hollers at one of them: a Hawaiian girl with platinum blonde hair, tight half-shirt, pink shorts. She must be fresh out of high school. Your average rich preppy cheerleader type. She is busy talking on her cell phone to somebody about a party she missed over the weekend, sitting down with us but not even looking in our direction. Only one shopping bag at her side.

I recognize the other girl. She is the witchy goth girl who was in the bathroom with me the other night. About college-aged, dragonfly tattoos on her arms. She is coated in dust and grime, probably from crawling around in the ceiling. She doesn't say anything either, just lights a cigarette and exhales over her shoulder.

We wait for others, but nobody comes.

"There's probably no one else," I say.

"I agree," Brock says. "Just the ten of us."

"Perfect number of subjects for an experiment . . ." the black guy says.

"Okay," Brock takes the phone away from the preppy girl and turns it off. "Let's first go around the room and have everyone introduce themselves."

"Excuuuuse me," the preppy girl says to Brock. "Who the hell are you to hang up my phone?"

Brock's voice gets annoyed. "You can talk on your stupid phone after we're done here."

"I want to know what's going on," says the Jesus woman. "I want answers right now!"

"Look, I have a plan for this discussion so don't freakin' interrupt me." Brock flexes his muscles at everyone. "We'll introduce ourselves first and then discuss the situation after that. Got it? Okay, I'll go first. My name is Brock Snatcher. People who've seen me play football call me Brock Ballsnatcher." He nods proudly at himself and the gothic girl fake-yawns. "I work with John over there," points at me, "and I've been stuck here since Friday. I have no idea what's going on, but if we stick together and work as a team I'm sure we'll figure this thing out. Now you go, John."

"I'm John," I say.

Everyone is still staring at me. I shrug.

Brock looks at the witchy girl: "I'm Chloe. I work at Hot Topic. Been hiding in the crawlspace for the past few days. I don't know why I don't want to leave. I hate the mall. I hate all the people in the mall. I always want to leave."

The cowboy: "Name's Aaron. I'm fresh out of the Reserves and working on my uncle's ranch. Just came for some new jeans a couple days ago. Just a single pair of jeans. But I ended up gettin' stuck here like the rest of you all. I'm a very strong-willed fella. I go to church, you know. But I still couldn't get myself to leave this place."

The black guy: "Spyder. I'm studying to be a game designer. I just got here this morning and was playing the display Xbox at Game Wizard when everyone disappeared. Nobody was around, so I put a couple games in my pants and walked out. But I didn't get out of the mall. I couldn't leave. I thought it was guilt holding me back so I returned the games. Then I ran into you guys. Looks like it's much more serious than I thought. So you've all been sleeping here every night? Hiding? That's nuts."

The white gangster kid: "Call me C-dogg, yo."

"C-dogg?" Spyder asks. "What's your real name?"

The kid looks down. "Cedrik."

"You look like a Cedrik," Spyder says.

Cedrik's face gets red. "Don't dis me, yo, we're bruthas."

"Brothers?"

"I'm like 30% black, yo," he says.

Spyder says, "Could've fooled me."

"Let's get back to business," Brock interrupts.

The Jesus woman: "I'm Carole. I run Christian Supply and have been sleeping there after closing each day since Friday. It feels like the apocalypse is coming. I'll pray for us."

The old man: "I don't know who any of you are. I wish you'd stop looking at me like that."

The mother: "My name is Wyoming and . . . And I'm never going to see my children again!"

The preppy girl: "I'm Jen and I want my fucking phone back, like right now."

Brock tosses the phone at her and it bounces off of her lap and smacks on the floor.

"What's your problem, asshole!" Jen squeals.

Brock holds up a notebook. "I want to hear ideas for getting out of here. We're going to try everything. Whatever it takes. I'm sure if we put our minds together we can come up with something."

He puts the notepad on his crossed leg and uncaps a pen, waiting for our suggestions. Nobody speaks.

"Well . . ." he says.

We look at each other.

"Somebody has to have some kind of idea . . ."

Nothing.

"We could . . . just walk through the doors. And leave," Spyder says.

"That's not going to work," Brock says.

"Why not?" Spyder asks.

"We've been trying that for days. None of us have been able to get out. You don't know. You just got here today."

"You think you can't leave," Spyder says. "But you really can. There's nothing physically stopping you. It's all in your head. I'm telling you, they brain-washed us."

"Nobody brain-washed us," Brock says. "It's not a conspiracy."

"Then what is it?"

"I . . . don't know. It just is what it is."

"It's a test," the Jesus woman says. "God's testing us."

"We could debate this all day," Brock says. "Personally, I don't care. I just want to figure a way out of here. We need to call for help or something."

"Do you really think anyone will help us?" Spyder says. "They look like they can't get inside any more than we can't get outside."

"There's got to be a way," Brock says.

"I don't think I want to leave," Chloe says.

Blank faces at her.

"Why leave?" she says. "We have the entire mall to ourselves. It's like Dawn of the Dead. We can do whatever we want in here, away from the zombies of the outside world."

"I don't want to leave either, yo," Cedrik says. "This place is tight like a bizike."

"What the fuck's a bizike?" Jen asks.

"Look, we can't stay here," Brock says. "Everything we eat we have to pay for. We can't steal food or anything else. Otherwise, we're going to end up in jail after we get out of here."

"And what happens if we never get out of here?" Chloe asks.

"Sooner or later we'll leave," Brock says. "Even if we have to tear the walls down."

CHAPTER THREE

Brock doesn't want to waste any time. After we leave our seats, he gets us to work on finding a way out. Thunder-clapping his hands to get us moving. He doesn't come up with any ideas himself, but gets mad at us when our minds draw a blank.

We check every exit first. They're all the same. Emergency exists, employee entrances, we can't go through any of them. Spyder thought we could get down from the roof, but we're not able to get on the roof. We found a door to it. It is unlocked. But none of us would open it.

We try pushing Aaron through the Nordstrom's east entrance, but our muscles go slack before we get him anywhere near it and his body takes on a mind of its own and resists us, flapping his arms and struggling to get away from us.

It's useless.

Spyder stands in front of one of the west entrances, trying to will himself through. His face flushed and legs shaking. He looks like I did two days ago.

Everyone gives up helping Brock look for a way out, except for Aaron and I. Wyoming is following us around, but doesn't help at all. She just cries a lot.

"We're running out of options," Brock says.

"Only one option left," Aaron says out of the side of his mouth.

"Call for help?" Brock asks.

"Yep."

"John, go find that girl with the cell phone and call 9-1-1 or whoever you can get a hold of," Brock says. "We'll call from upstairs."

I nod and they run off, Brock smacking Aaron's ass to get him going.

I find the preppy girl in the food court with Chloe and C-dogg. They are smoking a joint and Cedrik is stoned to the point of nausea.

"Have you like ever even smoked pot before?" Jen asks.

"I'm the pot masta, yo," Cedrik says. "Blunts for liiiife, nigga!"

"What the hell's wrong with him?" Chloe asks.

"We should do a threesome, yo," Cedrik mumbles, head spinning. "Either of you honeys wanna ride my wang?"

"Eeeeewww," Jen cries. "You're such a little perv."

"Once you go black you never go back, yo," Cedrik says, throwing a soggy gang sign.

"Are you really part black?" Jen asks.

"I'm like 60% black, yo," Cedrik says.

"This kid needs to die," Chloe says.

They don't seem to realize I'm here. I sit down next to Jen and pick up her cell phone.

Before I can dial a number, her wavy head jerks into sobriety at me.

"What the hell do you think you're doing?" she asks.

"We've got to call for help," I say.

She rips the phone out of my hand. "Nobody better touch my phone ever again, I swear."

"It's our only hope of getting out of here," I say.

"Fine," she says. "I'll call for help. I'll call Laney, she'll get us out of here."

She hits speed dial 3 and the first thing she says to her friend is, "Oh my god, I am so stoned right now. You would die, I swear."

Her conversation goes on for about an hour. Chloe leaves. Cedrik falls asleep. She doesn't say a word to her friend about our situation. Then she hangs up.

"Well?" I ask.

"Well, what?"

"You were supposed to call for help."

"Oh yeah, I forgot. Can you believe it? I'll call back."

She dials again. She says, "Oh my god, you have to see the new skirt I just bought . . ."

"Tell her to help us!" I say.

"Don't get an attitude," she says. "I'm not totally stupid, you know."

Then she talks to her friend, "Sorry, there's this guy being a total creep next to me. Can you believe it?" She goes on to talk with her friend about a party next weekend and which guy she'll impress with her new outfits. She ends the conversation without ever asking for help.

"Did you forget again?" I ask.

"Forget what?" she asks.

"You're supposed to call for help," I say. "Call your parents."

"I'm not calling my parents. Who the hell are you anyway?"

"Let me borrow the phone," I say.

"You touch my phone again and I'll . . ." she holds up a bottle of pepper spray from her key chain. "I swear."

"Just call somebody for help," I say. "I'm going crazy."

"Okay, okay," she says. "God. Okay? I'll call Laney again."

I meet up with Aaron and Brock in front of Lady Foot Locker.

"Any luck?" I ask.

They shake their heads.

"I can pick up the phone," Brock says. "I hear the dial tone. But my fingers won't dial out. It works when I call any store within the mall, but I can't dial 9-1-1. I can't call any of my friends or family."

"I tried the pay phones and the internet cafe," Aaron says. "I'm unable to do anything."

"Jen can call out of the mall," I say. "But she doesn't seem to be able to ask anyone for help. She just goes on and on about trivial things."

Brock shakes his head. Soft voice, "I don't know."

"There's nothing we can do," Aaron says.

"Let's just get something to eat," Brock says.

Spyder has worked at both S'barro's and McDonald's before, so he is able to make food for us. He says he can probably figure out how to cook food at the other restaurants in the mall, too. The rest of us are very happy we don't have to help.

"I tell you," Chloe says, "we should just enjoy ourselves while we can."

"She's right." Brock sighs. His shirt is off and he's rubbing the muscles on his chest. "There's nothing we can do."

Chloe smiles at him.

"We're never going to get out of here." Wyoming's eyes are plumped and crispy. "I'll never pick my children up from school again. I'll never get to make my husband dinner."

"We'll get out eventually," Brock says. "But we're stuck for now."

"My beautiful Honor Roll kids," Wyoming cries. "My rich doctor husband . . ."

Aaron hushes her and rubs her hair out of her eyes, his arm around her and cowboy hat shading her face.

"I don't know about the rest of you," Spyder says. "But I need a drink."

"Yeah," I say.

"I think we all could use a drink," Brock agrees.

"Heyll yeah," Cedrik says, rolling his head around and raising the roof.

Chloe punches him on the arm and he sinks into his chair.

At the Chili's bar, Spyder pours himself a glass of scotch and sighs.

"Get me a Bud Light," Brock says.

"Yeah, me too," I say.

"And me," Aaron says.

"Bud Light?" Spyder asks. "You know you can have anything you want?"

"Bud Light," Brock says.

"They've got all kinds of good beer," Spyder says. "Micro brews, Fat Tire, Sam Adams, Harp."

"Bud Light," Brock says.

"Yeah, Bud Light," Aaron says.

I don't know why Spyder is getting upset over this. Everyone drinks Bud Light. What's his problem? He nearly collapses when Jen and Wyoming want Bud Light as well.

"Got any malt liquor?" Cedrik asks.

"No, this is a bar," Spyder says. "They don't serve 40s here."

"How 'bout Mad Dowg 20/20?" Cedrik asks.

"No."

"No Maad Dowwwwg? Shiiiit, nigga. Gimme a Bud Light then."

Spyder doesn't even look at him when he gives him the beer. He sighs with relief when the goth girl asks for merlot.

"We need some music," Cedrik says to Spyder. "Put on some P Diddy, yo."

"Fuck that," Spyder says.

"You're right," Cedrik says. "2Pac is better."

"I hate rap," Spyder says.

Cedrik doesn't understand him.

"You're black and you don't like rap?" Aaron asks, out of the side of his mouth, amazed.

"Then what do you listen to?" Brock asks.

"I listen to punk and metal," Spyder says.

We all think he's joking.

"No, seriously," Brock says. "Blues? Reggae? What?"

Spyder grabs the bottle of scotch.

"I'm fucking surrounded by stereotypes," he cries, charging out of the bar.

At the end of the night, we stagger through the mall, our voices echoing back at us. There's just six of us now. The old guy and Wyoming disappeared at some point. Spyder never came back. And that Jesus freak woman nagged at us about our sins for three hours before going back to her store.

"This place doesn't seem real," I say to the goth girl. "It's like some kind of dream."

"I feel like we're ghosts," she says. "We died and will spend eternity haunting the mall."

We go into Dillard's and collapse onto the escalator. Everything's still running.

"Hold on," Chloe says to me, pulling me away from the escalator before I can ascend. "Can you wait for me? I want to change my clothes."

"Sure," I say.

She gets rid of her torn/filthy witch dress and walks through the store in black underwear. Her skin is as white as paper, black tattoos of dragonflies and Celtic knots on her arms, large demon wings on her back, spider and webs on her ribcage.

I get embarrassed when she catches me staring at her pale skin and look away. She snickers at me as she pulls on new clothes.

"Okay," she says, now wearing baggy orange pajamas.

They look designed for little kids. She leaves her dress where she dropped it.

Up the escalator, we find the others asleep in the display beds. There are only four of them. None left for us.

"Let's try another store," she says.

Walking through the mall in her pajamas.

"It feels like a slumber party," she says.

We can hardly walk by the time we make it to Sears. In the bedroom display, Chloe takes the bed that faces the aisle. It's designed to resemble an entire room.

"Good night," I tell her. "I'll be in a bed over there."

"No," she says. "I feel kind of weird in here by myself. Think you can sleep closer?"

"The other beds are over there," I say.

"We can share this bed. It's big enough for three or four."

"I don't know . . ."

"Please?" Her face is like a little kid's, matching her bright orange pajamas but contrasting with her black makeup.

I agree, but first pick out some pajamas for myself and wash the smell out of my crotch in the bathroom sink. Leaving my filthy clothes in the bathroom but keeping my shoes and wallet.

In bed with Chloe, she's still drunk and giggling. My head is beginning to hurt.

"What are we supposed to do about the light?" I say.

"There's probably a light switch somewhere," she says.

"I don't really want to go look for it," I say.

"Neither do I," she says.

"It's so bright," I say.

"Here." She pulls the cover over our heads. It's still not that dark but at least there's not a light shining directly into my eyes.

We look at each other under the cover and she laughs and says goodnight. She falls asleep facing me. Her cheek scrunched against the pillow, mouth open, lipstick smearing on the sheets, snoring softly. It takes me a while, but I eventually fall asleep to her breath against my forehead.

I wake to Brock kicking the bed.

"What's going on?" I ask him. "We having breakfast?"

"Wyoming's dead," he says.

I get up. Chloe is missing.

"She killed herself." His arms are crossed, shirt off, flexing his pecs in rhythm with his words.

"What?"

"She fucking hung herself from the second story railing with a jump rope. Right in front of K-B Toys."

"Killed herself?" I rub the crusties from my eyes, clear the snot from my throat.

"Didn't she have a family?" I ask.

"She wasn't in her right mind," he says, and punches a hole in the cardboard wall of the bedroom display.

She is still hanging up there. Nobody bothered to cut her down. Hair in her face.

"We should have tried to help her," I say.

"What could we've done?" Brock asks.

"Told her it wasn't hopeless, that we'd get out of here."

"How was I supposed to know she was going to kill herself?"

Barking dogs echo through the mall. We leave the dead woman and find some of the others around the corner, playing with puppies that they took from the Pet Pad. Wyoming's death doesn't seem to phase them a bit.

"I forgot all about the animals," Brock says.

I go to Chloe, now wearing a burgundy button up shirt and black vinyl pants, holding an American Eskimo.

"Isn't he cute?" she says.

I nod. Aaron and Jen are tossing a Bassett back and forth, and the Jesus freak woman is making baby kissing noises to a poodle-terrier.

"I don't want these fucking mutts running around the mall," Brock says. "You can take them out of the cages to play with, but don't let them loose. They'll shit all over the place."

Chloe sticks her tongue out at him.

"We're going to have to take care of them," I say. "Somebody has to feed them and clean their cages."

"We'll make jobs for everyone later," Brock says. "Some of us will cook, some will clean, some will take care of the animals."

"I do not clean cages," Jen says.

"Fine," Brock says. "I'll shoot the puppies so you won't have a job to do."

He walks away. Chloe's American Eskimo growls at him.

Chloe goes back to sleep and Brock wants to watch television in the Sears electronics department, so I don't know who to hang out with.

I go to the movie theater. The only movie that I have yet to see is called "28 Days Later." I heard the movie was terrible. They advertised it as the big hit horror movie of the summer, but everyone says that it's slow and doesn't have any computer animated effects or popular actors. I wish one of the Scream movies was playing instead. Those movies are really good.

Instead of 28 Days Later, I go into the T3 theater to see that one again. I'd rather see a movie that I know is going to be good than take a risk. Even if I've already seen the movie before.

The film is supposed to start in fifteen minutes or so. I sit in the back row of the theater and watch the commercials that are being projected. I love how they play commercials in the theaters these days. It reminds me of watching television on a very large screen. I laugh out loud at the commercials they play. I've seen all of these commercials a dozen times at home, but they are very funny to watch on the big screen. There are eight commercials total. When all eight have been played, they start over. I watch all of the commercials five or six times each, but I laugh at all the funny ones every time. I can't help myself. They're so funny!

After half an hour, I realize there's no projectionist to start the movie. The commercials are being repeated automatically. I watch the commercials a few more times and then leave the theater with a big smile on my face. All cheered up. I didn't even need to see a movie, heading to the food court to get a drink at Orange Julius.

"Everyone meet back at the food court," Brock's voice over the intercom. "I got some new information. Everyone meet back at the food court."

Not everyone meets at the food court. We wait for half an hour, drinking several orange drinks, but there's only five of us here: Brock, myself, Jen, Spyder, and Cedrik.

"They mentioned our problem on the news," Brock says.

"Really?" Jen asks. "We're on TV? Laney's going to die!" Opening her cell phone to dial.

"They didn't say anything about us," Brock says. "I don't even think they know about us. But they did mention something interesting."

"Like what?" Spyder is very hungover.

"The mall is menstruating," Brock says.

"What?" we ask.

"The mall is bleeding," he responds. "Blood is pouring out of pipes. They didn't know what it was at first, but they ran some tests on it. It is menstrual blood."

"How is that possible?" I ask.

"How is any of this possible?" Brock says.

"So what does that have to do with us being trapped here?" Spyder asks.

"Don't you get it?" Brock says. "The two must be connected. They said the mall started bleeding Friday. I've been trapped here since Friday. So . . ."

Spyder holds his headache in. "Just because two unexplainable events happen at the same time, that doesn't mean they have to be connected."

"It makes sense to me," I say.

"Why?" Spyder says. "The mall menstruating is some fucked up shit. Us not being unable to leave the mall for no reason whatsoever is some fucked up shit. But how can a mall menstruating stop us from walking out of here?"

"I don't know how the blood is causing this," Brock says, "but I know they are related somehow. The news said that hundreds of people are camped outside, waiting to get into the mall. But everyone is too frightened and disturbed by the menstrual blood to enter. I think once the mall stops menstruating we'll be able to leave."

"Oh really!" Jen cries. "That shouldn't take long at all then!"

"I know," Brock says. "It's period started Friday, so it should be over by . . ."

"Tomorrow!" Jen cries.

"It's almost over," Brock says. "We have just one more night here."

Spyder nods in agreement, almost in tune to Cedrik's head bobbing behind him.

"And we have to make sure to watch our behavior until then," Brock says. "We'll probably have to deal with the cops and God knows who—"

He is cut off by Chloe running into the food court. She stops at the counter of Panda Express, catching her breath.

We wait for her to speak, but it takes her a few minutes to cough tobacco smoke out of her lungs.

Then she says, "He's dead!"

Aaron is lying face down in the cowboy store with a large hunting knife in the back of his neck. A strong scent of rawhide in the air. And on the wall, there is something written in blood:

all the mundanes must die

"This one's no suicide." Brock flexes his neck at me and faces the others. "There's a killer among us."

CHAPTER FOUR

Brock tells us not to touch the body or anything in the store.

"The cops will investigate tomorrow," he says.

We race through the mall to look for the others, to make sure everyone else is all right. We find Carole behind the counter at her store.

"She looks all right," Brock says.

But before we can get into her shop, she pulls out a shotgun and fires at us. Scattering plexi glass into our faces.

"Don't come near me, sinners!" she screams. "I'm not letting you kill me too!"

She fires again, into the ceiling. She doesn't seem like she wants to hit any of us.

"Fucking psycho," Chloe says.

She fires again, through a display of Bible Man action figures to her right.

"Let's get out of here," Brock says.

We're out of her range of fire. Two more shots echo through the mall. Her voice shrieks the word "sinners" over and over again.

Back in the food court, the old guy is sitting at a table like he's been waiting for us there. He has his wicked smile and crooked eye staring straight ahead, at nothing.

"Did she kill him?" I ask Brock.

"I don't think it was her," Chloe says. "She probably saw Aaron's body and went nuts, especially after Wyoming hung herself."

"If she really did hang herself . . ." Spyder says.

"I don't know," Brock replies. "The woman is obviously insane, whether she killed them or not."

"What about the note?" I say. "It said 'all mundanes must die,' didn't it?"

"What the fuck's a mundane, yo?" Cedrik asks.

"Everyone listen to me," Brock says. "There's a killer in here somewhere. It's probably one of us. Somebody who thinks the rest of us aren't special and unique enough."

"Who do you think it is?" I ask Brock.

"One of the two of you," Brock says, looking straight at Spyder.

Cedrik, who happens to be sitting next to Spyder, throws some gang signs at Brock.

"What the fuck, yo?" Cedrik says. "You think we did it just because we're black?"

"He's not talking about you," Spyder says to Cedrik. "You're about as mundane as they come." His eyes cold. "He's talking about me and Chloe."

"Damn right I am," Brock says. "You were the one calling us mundane stereotypes last night."

"I didn't use the word mundane," Spyder says.

"Want me to punch you?" Brock says, holding up a flexed fist. "I know your types. You hate us because we fit in, because we conform and follow trends, but I bet I'm more of a nonconformist than you."

Spyder says, "Your logic is flawed."

"Why's that?" Brock says.

"Because the killer can just be pretending to be mundane," Spyder says. "You are all so stereotypical that I think you're joking half the time, pretending to be the way you are. The white boy gangsta, the snobby rich girl, the bible-thumper. Are you all for real? There's not a unique individual among you."

"Except for me," Chloe says.

"You?" Spyder tosses his blue dreads over his shoulder.

"You're a goth who shops at Hot Topic, for Christ's sake."

"I said I work there," Chloe says. "Who said I shop there?"

"Well, don't you?"

"Well, yeah, but only because—"

Spyder cuts her off, "You're as mundane as they come." Then he turns to the rest of us. "I'm telling you the killer is in disguise. And I have no idea who it is because you all seem like badly-written B-movie characters to me."

Chloe drops her head on my shoulder and I hold her hand, trying to comfort her. The two deaths don't seem to bother her much, but Spyder's words were thoroughly upsetting.

"The killer has to be one of us," Brock says. "Whichever one of you is the killer, I have a message for you."

Brock stands out of his chair and takes off his shirt, sucking in his stomach and flexing his pecs.

"Is that your message?" Spyder asks.

"Fuck you," he says, and then faces the rest of us. "I believe that everyone is a unique individual. Stereotypes don't really exist. The reason why people think stereotypes exist is because they don't take the time to get to know each other and jump to conclusions about a person's personality out of laziness. But people can't be categorized. We are all different and interesting in our own ways."

"Yes, we know you're very interesting," Spyder says.

Brock doesn't even bother responding to the comment. He continues, "So I want to go around the room and have each person tell the killer something interesting about themselves. Something to prove to him," he looks at Spyder, "that we're all not mundane stereotypes."

"What if the Jesus woman is the killer?" I ask.

"She's insane," Brock says. "If she's the killer she won't listen to reason no matter how interesting we are."

"Unless she's just putting on a show," Spyder says.

"Who goes first?" Brock asks. "I went first last time, somebody else go first."

Nobody says anything.

"Come on," he says. "I know you're all unique individuals on the inside. What makes you interesting?"

We look at each other. Jen is thinking really hard.

"Anything then," Brock says. "Anything interesting at all. There's got to be something hidden away inside you, even if it's something you're ashamed of."

Silence.

"I'm telling you," Spyder says. "Walking talking stereotypes, all of them."

"Then tell us about yourself," Brock says to Spyder. "You think you're so damn special. Prove it to me."

"I don't have to prove anything to anybody," Spyder says. "I am who I am. And what I'm not is mundane. I'm not the killer, but I sure as hell won't be a victim with you around."

"Just tell us one thing," Brock says. "One interesting thing."

"Christ," Spyder says, lowering his head and shaking his dreads, trying to search his mind for the right thing to say.

"Okay, here's something," he says, he looks at us. "I have a pedal-pumping fetish."

"A what?" I ask.

"I get off by watching girls' feet when they drive."

"Eeewww," Jen whines. "You like feet?"

"It's not just a foot fetish," his face is getting red. "It's about seeing a girl push gas into the engine. I don't know how to describe it. It's the combination of foot fetish and machine fetish."

"You're joking, right?" I ask. "There's no such thing as a machine fetish."

"There's a fetish for everything," Spyder says. "Rule 34."

"You think that makes you interesting?" Brock says.

"I don't know anyone else with that fetish," Spyder says. "Offline at least. Have you?"

"Fine," Brock says. "Who else?"

He points to the old guy. "What about you?"

The old man is wickedly grinning into space.

"What makes you interesting and unique?" Brock asks.

He doesn't stop his smile and blank stare. He pops out his glass eye and holds it up to us.

"Ahh," Brock says. "He has a glass eye. See that? That's interesting!"

The old man isn't done yet. He pulls a wad of hair out of the eye hole.

"Eeewwww," Jen whines. "What is thaaaat?"

The old man caresses the hair wad in his hand.

"It's my pet," the old man says, stroking the tiny crusty ball.

"Is that hair?" Brock asks.

The old man nods.

"It took me a year to make him," he says. "I collected hair from every public toilet seat in the mall and pressed them together. He lives in my face like a cave." He holds up the glass eye. "This is his door."

"It's pubic hair?" Brock cries.

Everyone sitting next to him leaps out of their seats and dashes behind Brock. The preppy girl hops up and down, fanning her head with her palms.

"Now that's just plain wrong, but it's interesting," Brock says, laughing. "He's not a stereotypical old man. He's too perverted to be."

"But doesn't he fit the perverted old man stereotype?" Spyder asks.

Brock ignores him.

The old man shuts his pet back in its cave and goes back to wicked-grinning.

"Who's next?" Brock asks. "Everybody has to say something even if it's not that interesting."

The rest of us take our turns . . .

Jen: "I have three cars. Know any other 18-year-old with three cars? I don't think so! I won Little Miss Scottsdale when I was nine and I lost my virginity to Todd Hooper, Chaparral High's star quarterback. Can you believe it?"

Cedrik: "Even though I look like I'm white, yo, I'm really like 80% black. I'm like a unique and interesting case, ya know what I'm sayin? Somehow the 20% of me that's white is what ya see on the outside, yo. But on the inside I'm 100% brutha, know what I'm sayin? And my dick is fuckin big, yo. It's HUGE. Know what I'm sayin? Thug life, nigga!"

Chloe: "There's nothing mundane about me. I've written two novels, a short story of mine was published, I've been the singer of a riot grrrl band, I've thrown a rave in my neighbor's basement without him knowing about it, I have a blood fetish, five tattoos, I'm going to get fangs implanted into my mouth, I read almost a hundred books a year, I make my own clothes, I've attempted suicide twice, I've tried every drug in existence, I've had a threesome, I've had an abortion, my favorite animals are crabs and snails, and I think pickled sausage is the best food ever. I am far far from ordinary."

She is out of breath after that, pouting with a red face. It was like she had something to prove and still doesn't believe that she's proved it yet.

Everyone looks at me. It's my turn. I still can't think of anything interesting about me. I think back to my childhood.

"My dad shot himself when I was nine," I say.

Pause. They're all eying me.

"I was in the next room when it happened, playing with my favorite He-Man action figures. He was arguing with himself and crying. It wasn't anything unusual at first, but then a bullet came through the wall and landed in Castle Grayskull. It still had blood on it.

"My mother told me it was an accident. I never believed her. She turned into another person after that. An apathetic person. She drank herself to death over the next ten years. After she died, I didn't feel any more alone than when she was still alive. But I realized that I was, and had always been, alone. I was an only child. Both of my parents were also only childs. And all of their parents had died before I was born. I had no family. No friends either, at least none that I felt close to. Fresh out of high school, a legal adult, completely and utterly alone in the world."

I want to say more, but I can feel a pain in my throat. Like I'm about to cry.

"Now that is interesting," Brock says. "See, everyone has something unique about them. Something extraordinary."

He composes himself. "Take me . . ."

It's his turn. He rubs sweat from his chest and slicks back his hair with it.

"I've never told this to anyone in my life . . ."

He takes a deep breath.

"But I want the killer to know that I am an interesting, unique person. Not some mundane stereotype."

He takes another deep breath.

"The thing that makes me unique and different is . . ."

His eyes close.

"I'm gay."

He opens his eyes.

"I've never told that to anyone before," he says. "It's been bottled up inside of me since the eighth grade, but now I'm telling you. Even though I'm very strong and masculine, I'm a homosexual man."

He reaches over and pats me on my knee, to show me he feels for my sad story.

"Is that it?" Spyder asks.

"What do you mean?" Brock asks.

"You're gay?" Spyder asks. "That's the thing that makes you interesting?"

Brock gets angry, "Hey, I—"

"Do you know how many gay people there are?" Spyder says. "There's more gays in this country than there are blacks. Do you think I'm an interesting person just because I'm black?"

"But listen—" Brock tries to say.

"And John," Spyder turns to me, "it's a sad story and all, but just because your parents are dead it doesn't mean you're not mundane. Everyone's parents die eventually. My dad died last year. It's very tragic that they died when you were young, but it could have happened to anybody. It doesn't change who you are as a person. It still makes us perceive you as nothing but an office monkey."

"I swear you're the murderer," Brock says, aiming a fist at him.

"I'm not the killer," Spyder says. "I'm just trying to point out that being gay in itself does not make you unique and interesting."

"You homophobe!" Brock says to him.

"Race traitor!" Cedrik says to him.

Spyder hits his head into his fists and screams.

I'm not sure what's wrong with him.

"Are we done here yet?" Chloe asks.

"No," Brock says. "Nobody's going anywhere."

Jen groans.

"The mall will be done menstruating tomorrow. We'll be able to leave then. If we all stay together the killer can't get any more of us. And we can let the police handle this when they get here."

Chloe crosses her legs. "So are we going to sleep in bed together? Shit together?"

"Nobody's leaving this spot," Brock says. "We're going to stay in these seats until the police get here. You can sleep on the floor or stay up all night, it doesn't matter. And if you need to shit you can do it in a bucket behind the Chick-fil-A counter."

"Are you like serious?" Jen asks.

"We just have one more night," Brock says. "Then we can get out of here."

We stay up all night and most of the next day. Every hour we check to see if we can leave, check to see if the rusty red liquid is still flowing, check to see if Jen can actually ask for help when she calls her friends. Nothing changes.

"Fuck it," Spyder says. "It's not going to end."

"It's going to any minute," Brock says.

"You're clueless," Spyder says. "A mall can menstruate for five months for all we know."

"Don't leave," Brock cries.

"I'm tired," Spyder says. "I'm going to sleep."

Everyone else leaves with him. There's an awful stink coming from behind the Chick-fil-A counter and I'm getting delirious. I decide it would be better not to go to sleep.

A scream wakes me. I must have fallen asleep on a bench.

Others are rushing to a body on the other side of the mall, near the eastern entrance. I go to them.

Jen is covering her mouth and trying not to scream again. Brock and Chloe are with her, examining the corpse. It is Carole, collapsed in front of the entrance with a metal crucifix jammed through the top of her skull. She's still warm, blood still dripping down her neck.

"She couldn't get out," Brock says. "She must've ran to the

exit but wasn't able to leave. All she had to do to escape the killer was open the door and walk out, but she wouldn't do it . . ."

"Look," Chloe says.

She pulls a piece of paper out from under the woman's dress.

The note reads:

break out of your mold and you will be spared

"What happened to her shotgun?" I ask.

Brock squeezes a fist.

"Fuck," he says. "It better be in her store."

"If the killer has it," Chloe says. "He can kill all of us at any time."

CHAPTER FIVE

Brock, Chloe, and I are hiding out in the Sam Goody, thinking about what we're going to do. Rap-metal blasting in the background. Brock insists that Spyder is the killer, but Chloe isn't too sure. She says it's more likely the old guy, but he isn't very agile. He couldn't have chased down the bible-thumper or taken down the big cowboy. But still, Chloe thinks there's something peculiar about the old man.

I can hardly keep my eyes open. Chloe's and Brock's words aren't making sense to me anymore. I sit down on the floor and try to stay awake.

My eyes close.

I open them. Brock is twisting his nipples and wiggling his hips.

I close my eyes again.

Chloe wakes me up and helps me get back to Sears. She puts me into the bedroom display and wraps herself around me.

"Can you help me break out of my mold?" I ask her in a daze.

"We'll see what happens," she says.

Most of her makeup smeared across her face onto mine.

As I drift away, she is saying something that I don't understand. Her lips wrap around the back of my neck and her teeth press against the skin. She falls asleep on me in this position. I awake a few hours later and drool is dribbling out of her mouth, down my shoulders, like blood.

In the morning, we eat McDonald's sausage biscuits for breakfast. Sunken faces. Shit smells in the air.

Nobody died during the night.

"He's giving us a chance to try to prove ourselves," Brock says. "All we have to do is break out of our molds and we'll be safe. It'll be easy."

So we decide to spend the entirety of the day trying to break out of our molds.

We don't know where to begin.

Cedrik and Jen don't even realize they're in a mold. They think that they just have to prove they are cool in some way. Jen shops for the most expensive and attractive clothes she can find. Cedrik raps over the intercom really badly. He mostly just repeats different variations of these three lines: 1) I'm da nigga wit da blunts and da hos. 2) I cap yo ass, bitch. 3) Drink my forty ounces of dick, yo.

At Chili's, drinking Bud Light:

"Just be spontaneous and crazy," Chloe says.

"But what do I do?" I ask.

"Do anything you'd never normally do," she says. "For starters, drink something besides Bud Light."

"What's wrong with Bud Light?" I ask. "It's my favorite beer. Why does Bud Light make me mundane?"

"Just try something new for a change," Chloe says.

She pours me another beer.

I taste it, my face crinkles. "Gross, what the hell is that?"

"IPA," she says.

"Bitter beer face!" I say and then laugh. Like that really funny commercial on TV.

"Try something else," she says, pouring me another beer. "This is the most expensive beer in the house."

Well, the most expensive beer will have to be excellent. I push away the IPA and try the new one. It's really good!

"Now this is a good beer, I can tell," I say.

"I lied," she says. "It's the cheapest beer in the place. Pabst Blue Ribbon."

"The cheapest?" I taste it again and spit it back out into the glass. "Gross, I hate cheap beer."

"You're hopeless," Chloe says.

She shakes her head and walks out of the bar.

I find Spyder in Game Stop, playing some Jedi Knight game on the Xbox. Noisy punk music in the background, but the lyrics are all in Spanish.

"What's up?" I ask him.

He keeps playing, doesn't respond. I watch him. He seems very good at killing storm troopers.

"I've beat this game six times since I've been here," Spyder says. "But I keep playing it. I'm not getting any sleep. Just playing this game. I can't stop."

"Is it fun?" I ask.

"I don't know," he says, still destroying storm troopers with his light saber. "I thought it was fun when I started, but now I've beaten it so many times it's too easy. But I can't stop. I can't play any other games. Just like I can't leave the mall."

I watch him play the game for a while.

"Games have always been my obsession," he says. "I know they are a complete waste of time. They're probably the biggest unproductive hobby you can have, but I just can't stop playing them. I dropped out of college three times because of these games. I was fired from two jobs. And I keep telling myself I play these games for research. I want to be a game designer. But who the fuck am I kidding? It's never going to happen."

"Why not?" I ask.

"I'm a mess," he says.

I watch him play the game for a while longer.

"There you are," Chloe calls to me, walking into Game Stop with new clothes over her shoulder. She is now wearing a shirt with a picture on it of some kind of cartoon character called Meat Wad. She's not wearing a bra.

"Let's try again," she says. "Put these clothes on. You need a new look."

"Okay," I say, as she pulls clothes out of a Hot Topic bag.

Spyder shakes his head at us. "You think having him wear clothes from Hot Topic is going to make him less mundane?"

"I'm trying to break him out of his mold," she says.

"Sounds to me like he's about to break out of one mold and step into another," Spyder says.

"It's just a start," she says. "The only store with cool clothes in this entire mall is Hot Topic. It'll at least be better than what he's wearing now."

Spyder shakes his head. "Your problem is that you try to be unique on the outside. But it's the inside that matters. That's what you should concentrate on."

Chloe grabs me by the wrist and pulls me out of the store. I feel like a little kid again.

Chloe gives me a very strange look. I'm wearing goth clothes, but I look more like something out of a mad max movie. She gives me three blue spiky Mohawks. They are each about two inches high. There are chains and straps dangling from me, attached from one part of my body to another, serving no purpose that I can fathom. She draws dragon scales on my skin with a felt-tip pen, like a full body tattoo. Then stitches forks and spoons to the back of my shirt and tapes a giant novelty schlong from Spencer's Gifts on my thigh, outside of the pants.

"So am I cool now?" I ask.

"I don't know about that," she says. "But you're definitely weird."

We go out and roam the mall. I feel like I'm one of her kind now. A weird person. I like the feeling. It's like I'm part of something exciting.

"Now what?" I ask.

"We have to go crazy," she says. "Do things we'd never normally do."

"Like what?" I say. "Urinate in the fountain?"

"Sure," she says.

"Or knock this garbage can over?" I push it over.

"Now you're talking," she says.

We get bottles of southern comfort and baseball bats from Sears and go on a smashing spree, running and screaming like lunatics, chugging the syrupy hard liquor, and hitting everything that looks breakable. We are like a tornado thrashing through the mall, knocking over benches, displays, water massage tables, a cart of hermit crabs, a pretzel stand.

Brock sees us and shakes his head, he's now in drag. A purple-flowered dress, red high-heels, pink lipstick, and a blond wig. Chloe splashes him with some southern comfort and belch-screams in his face.

We attack The Gap with buckets of paint, coating the clothes and the walls in black. It looks like a tar pit when we're through. Chloe breaks all of the cages at the Pet Pad and lets the animals free. Dogs and ferrets and rabbits and snakes and tarantulas scatter into the mall. I go to Waldenbooks and throw all of the books on the bestseller list into the fountain. The old man sitting nearby watches with his crooked eye and wicked grin.

At a jewelry store, we charge the glass displays, and smash them repeatedly. The shattering glass sounds are like music, striking in rhythm with each other.

Shards of glass prick my face. I cut my hand and stop smashing. Chloe stops smashing as well.

I look at her.

She is also cut, but very deep. Her arms are coated in blood, and she's licking it like a cat. I go to help her, but she doesn't seem hurt. She's enjoying it. Her eyes are wild, shivering. She looks ravenous.

"Fuck me," she says, looking at me with a bloody chin. "The blood!"

She sees my red hand and tries to drink from it, but the cut isn't very deep. She takes a large knife of glass and cuts it wider. I shriek as a gush of blood spurts into her mouth. She hisses a smile. I'm beginning to feel nauseous.

Ripping her Meat Wad shirt in half, she rubs my blood on her paper white breasts and bites my neck. She tears my shirt open and licks up the side of my face.

Hungry eyes staring at me, as she slides off her vinyl pants and bends over the glass counter. I don't have an erection. I'm in too much pain. She grabs my belt and pulls my crotch into her ass. I don't know what to do, so I kneel down and lick the back of her thigh. She laughs. It must tickle.

Her hands are digging into the shards of glass. She picks up her baseball bat and starts smashing again, the glass, the jewelry display, as I caress her hips and lick the backs of her legs. I finally get hard, but before I can stand up she grabs my head and forces it into her ass crack.

"Tongue," she screams.

I stick out my tongue against a white cheek and she maneuvers herself until it enters her asshole. I don't know what to do. This is definitely not something I would normally do, or would ever want to do, but I don't really have a choice. My life depends on it. I fuck her asshole with my tongue and she stops smashing the glass. Her breaths are heavy. I feel her fingernails on my chin. She's masturbating herself.

I stand up and unzip. Looking at her, she sticks her middle finger in her asshole, then her index finger, with the same hand she's masturbating with. Preparing herself for me. I've never done this before. She's about five years younger than me, but I feel like a child in comparison.

She howls when I fuck her, smashing everything in her reach with the baseball bat. I can feel her asshole squeeze-pumping around my cock when she orgasms. Then she pushes me out and puts it in her mouth.

She is a disturbing sight—on her knees, naked and bloody, staring up at me with crazy eyes while giving me an ass-flavored blow job. I'm not sure if it's sexy or disgusting, but I think I'm falling in love.

We slow down quite a bit, wash ourselves up in a bathroom, clean our wounds. No more baseball bats for us.

Strolling through the mall, holding our clothes together. I'm very proud of myself, smiling when Chloe isn't looking. There's no way I can be considered mundane after that.

"That was the craziest experience I've ever had in my life!" I say.

"It can get a lot crazier," she says.

The others are gathered at the end of the mall, by the fountain. I wonder what they thought about our little rampage.

I bet they're impressed.

When we get closer, we notice something is wrong.

"There's been another murder," Brock says, now wearing a black bikini, flexing his muscles at us.

We get to them, by the fountain full of books.

It's the old man. He's floating face-down inside of the fountain.

"No . . ." I say. "Not him."

The others are just standing in silence. Unable to speak.

"He was the weirdest of us all," Brock says. "If he was considered mundane, then we all have a very long way to go before we can break out of our molds."

"Not even Spyder is safe," I say.

CHAPTER SIX

Everyone is in the food court, sitting in silence.

"I don't know what to do," Jen cries. "I don't know how to be any more interesting than I already am."

She cries into Brock's bosom.

"The killer has a different definition of interesting than you do," Spyder says.

"We have to be as abnormal as possible," Chloe says. "Go nuts, do things we normally wouldn't do."

"You mean like what you've been doing all day?" Spyder says. "Vandalizing the mall makes you an interesting person?"

"Chaos is interesting," Chloe says. "Order is mundane."

"I'm not in the mood to run around and act like an idiot," Spyder says.

"Why not?" I ask. "It couldn't hurt."

Chloe says, "It's better than just sitting around, waiting to die."

"You all can do that," Spyder says. He stands out of his seat. "But I don't want any part of it."

The rest of the night is drunken chaos. Chloe feeds me shot after shot of hard liquor until my mind goes limp. I drift in and out of consciousness, hearing screams and crashing sounds. It's like I'm sleeping in the middle of a battlefield.

My eyes open. Cedrik is rapping right in my face, repeating a single line over and over again: "I'm down wit da drive-bys, drive-bys. Down wit da drive-bys, drive-bys." My eyes close. My eyes open. Brock, in a fluffy pink coat, is smashing the floor with a sledgehammer. My eyes close. My eyes open. Chloe is racing hamsters and guinea pigs across the floor. My eyes close. My eyes open. Chloe is pulling a tarantula off of my neck and giggling. My eyes close.

The next morning.

I wake up in the same bed display in Sears, next to an inflatable sex sheep instead of Chloe.

Wandering through Sears naked, looking for some new clothes. My mohawks are mostly flat now and the goth clothes are ruined. Time to find a new look.

I put on a pair of briefs. I haven't worn briefs in years.

"Screw it," I say, not bothering with any other clothes.

Minimalism is a style too.

The entire mall is trashed. Not just trashed, but pulverized. It looks like a bomb exploded in here, a post-apocalypse wasteland. Everything's been spray-painted, toilet-papered, sledgehammered, flipped over, burned, blown up, coated in food and gunk. Mountains of clothes, toys, and debris make it difficult to walk anywhere. Smoke is twisting out of a broken elevator. A stereo system is set up in the center court, blasting some kind of screechy violin music.

Walking barefoot, I try not to step on any glass or jagged chunks of metal. Nails are falling from the second story balcony like drops of rain. A smell like rotten cherries and hamburger helper spreads across my face.

Spyder is in front of the south entrance. His head down, in deep concentration. I go to see how he's doing, but he blocks me out. He's mumbling something to himself, like a chant.

Outside, there are still hundreds of people looking into the mall. Their faces blank and ghostly. They seem fake. Like cardboard cut-outs. I don't seem to care that they are looking at me in my underwear.

In the food court, also a devastated wood-splintery junkyard, Cedrik is building a fort out of hamburgers.

Brock is gawking over him. "You think this hamburger castle is really going to make you less mundane?"

"Fo' shizzle," Cedrik says, coated in mustard and grease.

Jen is coloring the surface of a table with crayola crayons. She's shaved her head and smashed her cell phone. Even her eyebrows have been shaved. She's not wearing makeup. Her clothes are made of feathers.

I go to Brock. He isn't in drag anymore.

"Can you believe them?" he asks me. "Fucking pawns."

We get cookies and coffee and sit down at a table.

"I'm not playing this game anymore," he says. "Yesterday was enough degradation to last me a lifetime."

He pounds his fist on the table. "Spyder's going down."

"You don't know he's the killer."

"He is. I know he is. I'm not going to kill him until he comes at me, but I know it's him."

He drinks from his coffee, a terrible smell emerges from under his arm. "He's coming for me next, and I'm going to be ready for him."

"Don't be so sure it's Spyder," I say. "I could be the killer for all you know."

"I know you," he says. "You're no killer."

"How do you know?" I say. "You don't know anything about me. We work together, but it's not like we've been friends."

"I know you," he says, squinting his eyes and nodding.

Time to go do something insane. I don't know how being insane breaks us out of our molds, but everyone else is doing it so I should too.

I'm hit in the kidney with a heavy rounded object and I crumble to the floor.

Turning around, clutching my back.

"Nice whitey-tighties," Chloe says.

She is standing above me, wearing nothing but football shoulder pads, a Viking helmet, and a homemade strap-on dildo. In her hands is a Klingon bat'leth that she just clubbed me with like a baseball bat. She used the blunt side, luckily, but now has the bladed side aimed at my neck.

"You fucked me in the ass," she says. "Now it's my turn."

Chloe and I fall in love today.

We spend the afternoon together, wandering through the mall-apocalypse terrain like lovers by a lake. I was in pain from the club in the kidneys and the anal-raping, but after a couple long island iced-teas I'm okay.

"It's like a paradise," she says, pointing at our surroundings with her bat'leth.

She kisses me on the nipple.

We go to see the 28 Days Later movie, hoping we'll be able to figure out how to run the projector. Chloe tells me that it's the only good movie this mall has played in years and that everyone who told me not to see it is retarded.

Upon entering the theater, we hear bubbling and squeaking noises in the darkness. Instead of commercials, the projector is playing an old silent movie. It makes a sound similar to a record player between songs.

A massive white blob is in the center of the room, taking up about four rows of seats. It looks like a mountain of lard.

I watch the movie from the door. It must be very old. The film is warped and gritty. On screen: there is a man staring at a hole in his hand. Dozens of black ants are crawling in and out of the hole. A flesh anthill. They creep around his fingers and down his wrist. Very little emotion on the man's face.

Chloe steps toward the white blob in front of us. I follow her. The mound seems like the texture of an eyeball, with animals sticking out of it.

Chloe yells in my ear, "They've gone too far."

All the pets from the Pet Pad have been cut into pieces and glued to the dome-like blob. The dogs, rabbits, mice, all of them. Somebody made a disturbing sculpture out of their body parts. Bubbles ooze from it, a white chocolate scent.

Chloe sees the head of the American Eskimo puppy she loved to play with. I think she is crying. The flashing movie in the darkness makes everything hard to see. She goes to the puppy and pets its forehead. It barks at her. The blob sculpture bursts into movement as the animal parts wiggle and bark and growl at us. She jumps back, knocking me over. Then lunges forward, slicing at the blob with her Klingon weapon.

On screen: a woman is trying to stop a man from getting into the room with her. She is slamming his arm in the door, but he won't stop. He is reaching for her with his ant-filled hand, desperate to get at her.

Chloe picks me up and pulls me out of the theater. Barking noises in the background and flashing white lights.

We try to forget about the animal sculpture with a few drinks.

Chili's has been turned into a swamp. Somebody must have flooded the toilets and sinks somehow, or messed with the plumbing. The sunken bar area is now submerged at least two feet in dark green liquid. We have to step carefully across stools and tables like rocks on a river, and sit on the counter of the bar like a picnic blanket.

Chloe rolls onto my lap and balances pretzels on her nose. She has the Klingon bat'leth tight between my legs.

"I'm not in love with you yet," she tells me. "But I want to be."

"What's holding you back?" I ask.

"With some work you can be my perfect boyfriend," she says. "You've already started to progress, but you're not there yet."

"I think I can change," I say.

She smiles at me and puts my chin in her palm. "I'm glad that you're trapped here forever."

"It won't be forever."

"It will," she says. "You know it will."

"How did somebody like you get trapped here?" I ask. "You're not like the rest of us."

She giggles at me.

"What?" I ask.

"I have a confession to make," she tells me.

Her face goes serious. She slips off of my lap and faces me. "I'm not really trapped here."

"What are you talking about?" I ask her.

"I lied about being unable to leave," she says. "I can leave any time."

"Why don't you leave then?" I ask.

"I've got no place else to go." She fidgets with her foot. "After my boyfriend kicked me out of our apartment, I decided to sleep up in the crawlspace above Hot Topic until he took me back. But after the first night, I decided I didn't want to go back to that controlling, abusive asshole. The crawlspace is amazing. There's a whole maze up there. I found a cozy area above the food court that I turned into a bedroom. I lived there for almost a year, hidden away, rent free. It's a quiet place where I'm able to concentrate on writing. I want to be the next Poppy Z. Brite. Have you read her? I've got a bed up there, a laptop, battery-operated lights, a ton of books. The only downside is that I have to clean myself with a sponge in the public bathrooms."

"But why don't you leave?" I ask.

"I haven't left the mall in months," she says. "This is my home. I like it here. I don't ever want to leave. The only thing I hated was the mall people, but they're all gone now. I don't need to hide in my secret room anymore. I have the whole mall."

"But Chloe," I say, "there's a killer on the loose. If you're able to leave, why don't you get out of here and save yourself?"

"I don't care about the killer." She gets angry with me. "I'm not afraid of him. This is my home, I'm not going to leave. Especially now that it's so fun and interesting. I'm not mundane, so I don't have anything to worry about."

Wait a minute, there's something strange about all this. She's not . . .

"You're the killer, aren't you?" I ask.

"Don't be stupid," she says.

"It all makes sense," I say. "You want to stay here, but you don't want to share the mall with mundanes like us. We have to either change or die."

"No," she cries. "I swear it's not me."

I push her as hard as I can. "Get away from me," and she falls off of the bar and into shelves of liquor bottles. The shelves collapse, glass shattering against her.

Flipping around, I jump into the swamp and splash through the toe-odorous liquid. As I get onto dry carpet, Chloe shrieks into my ear. Then my stomach explodes.

I look down . . . The Klingon bat'leth is inside of me, driven halfway through from the back. Blood and gore waterfalls down my legs, intestines dangling out.

My body tenses. I don't feel any pain.

Chloe wraps her arms around me and moans into my ear, caressing my bare chest and kissing my neck.

"It could have been so good," she says, pulling me back into the swamp with her.

Floating in the water, she grabs my penis out of my briefs and jerks me off as she drinks the blood from my stomach wound, sucks on a rope of intestine like a cock. She pulls off her pants and wet shirt, rubs her middle finger into her crotch, getting ready to mount me . . .

Everything fades.

CHAPTER SEVEN

I'm inside of the dark and slowly fading into consciousness. My eyes aren't open. I can't open them.

But I hear voices . . .

"I should've been next," Brock says. "Why the fuck didn't he come after me?"

"I can't believe he's dead," Chloe cries.

"This is fucked," Brock says. "Fucked!"

"Why was he killed?" Chloe cries. "He broke out of his mold! He became interesting!"

"Not interesting enough," Spyder says.

"Interesting?" Cedrik says. "He was a chump, yo."

I hear Cedrik hit the ground.

"He was more interesting than you'll ever be!" Chloe screams at the kid. "Asshole!"

She begins to cry.

"You have to be strong," Brock says, comforting Chloe. "We'll get through this, I promise."

I realize my eyes aren't closed. They are open, just black. The room is fuzzy, but it's starting to fade in.

I blink.

"Just five of us left," Spyder says.

Their figures come into focus a little better. I can see Brock holding Chloe in his arms as she cries into his pecs. Cedrik is bobbing his body around in the background, silently rapping to himself. Spyder stands in the foreground with a bottle of scotch.

My body is mostly numb, but I'm beginning to feel prickly sensations. Everything is wet. My lower body is underwater, but my torso and head are held up by the bat'leth in my back.

"What's going on?" I ask them.

They freeze.

"I don't think I can get up," I say.

"Holy fuck, he's alive!" Brock says.

"Daaaaaamn!" Cedrik says.

Spyder splashes into the water next to me.

"Don't move," Spyder says. "Whatever you do, don't move."

My vision is back to normal. I can see Chloe backing away. Her mouth wide open, too shocked to keep up her act.

"Tell us," Spyder says. "Who is the killer? Who did this to you?"

I pause, my eyes roll. I try to stand up.

"No," Spyder cries, holding me into place so that I can't move. "You don't understand the condition you're in. Moving just an inch could kill you."

"Quickly." Brock enters the water. "You have to tell us who it is. Who did you see?"

My eyes roll again.

I try to speak, but Spyder interrupts me, "Fucking tell us now!"

I look over Brock's shoulder at Chloe, look into her eyes. She is staring back at me. She cries again, but this time for real. And not for me.

"Come on, come on," Brock says, like he can physically see my life's hourglass running out, as if there's just a few grains of sand left.

"I don't remember," I say.

They punch their fists into the water at me.

"Remember, damn it!" Brock says.

"Concentrate," Spyder says.

I pretend to search my brain.

"I don't know who it is," I tell them. "I think I was attacked from behind. I blacked out."

They buy it, but they aren't very happy with me.

"Fucking hell!" Brock says, storming out of the bar.

Cedrik and Spyder walk out as well, knowing that I'm going to die at any second, leaving me alone with Chloe.

She enters the water with slow and careful steps.

Her clothes are different. She's wearing a black skirt, fishnet stockings, a mesh shirt, and a black bikini top with skulls and crossbones on the breast cups. I didn't notice her wearing the outfit before. She must have changed them to get rid of her wet bloody clothes. Her hair is still soggy though, slicked back, flat to her head. I wonder why nobody realized that her hair is wet. The killer obviously attacked me in this murky pool. Hasn't a single one of them heard of deductive reasoning?

Chloe's eyes are locked on me, approaching like a snake. She stands over me, then squats down into my lap. The bat'leth blade under her skirt.

"Why didn't you tell them about me?" she asks.

Her eyes are wide at me. I never noticed how beautiful they are, how unique. They normally look brown, but this close I can see a thin ring of green with hints of blue and a purple spiral-like shape near the pupil. I've never seen anything like it before.

I smile at her. My bloody face staring back at me in her eyes.

"Because I love you," I tell her.

Chloe smiles and kisses me, deeply.

Her voice is soft. "I'm sorry." Big wet eyes at me, making them even more alluring.

"It's my fault," I tell her, as she rapid-kisses my face and neck. "I gave you no choice. I didn't know what I was doing."

"I don't want you to die," she says. "I'm so sorry."

I wipe a tear from her cheek with my bloody hand.

"Hurry," her voice now stern. She stands and pulls her underwear off, still wearing her black skirt. "I need you. There's not much time left."

We make love gently. Our eyes locked, trapped in each other's stare. I can feel her emotions surging from her skin, can almost see them, as she carefully slides me in and out of her. Even though there's this crudely bladed weapon sticking out of my stomach, keeping us from pressing our upper bodies together, I have never felt more close to a human being. It is her apology and farewell. She wants to make it perfect for me.

When I come, it feels like I've emptied my lifeforce into her. Every particle of my essence drains out of my body and fills her cunt. She knows it too. Her eyelids snail down over her eyes, concentrating on me, relishing the sensation of having captured me inside of her. And she smiles wickedly as her body absorbs my spirit, making me a part of her, forever.

She wraps herself around my back with my skull in her chest, the bat'leth between her legs. Waiting for me to die.

I do not die.

A solemn embrace for a few hours until we get sick of shriveled fingers and backaches. But I'm still not dead for some reason. In fact, I don't feel all that bad.

"I'm going to try to get up," I say.

Chloe doesn't argue. She springs out of the water to help.

My legs are a little stiff, but I'm able to stand up fine. I stretch my legs and walk in a circle. No problems.

I examine the Klingon weapon inside of me. There's still no pain at all. It feels as if it's supposed to be here. I'm no longer bleeding, but my stomach is a goopy red mess. A few intestines are dangling out, tickling my crotch. I try to stuff them back in, but the bat'leth is in the way. I try to move the weapon, but it doesn't budge.

"Let me try," Chloe says.

She pulls on the bat'leth, but my body goes with her.

"One more time," she says.

She lifts a foot into the back of my shoulder, and shoves off of me with the weapon in hand. It doesn't come free. Her hand slips off of the handle.

"That thing's going nowhere," she says.

She giggles uncontrollably, very happy all of a sudden. Perhaps it is dawning on her that I'm not going to die anytime soon. Or perhaps she's just laughing at how stupid I look with this thing stuck through my torso.

We search for some new clothes for me. Chloe doesn't want to have to look at the gore hanging out of me anymore, so we need to cover it up somehow. She puts a black button-up shirt on me, stabbing the bat'leth through the back and buttoning around it in the front.

She laughs at me again.

"I like it!" she says, hopping and smiling.

I respond to her cheerful mood with apathy.

"What's wrong with you?" she asks.

I shake my head.

"What?" she asks, kissing me on the bat'leth.

"Promise me you won't kill anyone else," I say.

She stops smiling.

"I'm serious. If you kill anyone else I'm going to tell them about you."

"How could you do such a thing?" she asks, her eyes getting glossy.

"There's no reason to kill anyone else," I say. "Everyone is doing all they can to be less mundane. They don't need any more of your morbid incentives."

She frowns at me like a child denied of a puppy.

"Do you promise?" I ask.

She bites her tongue at me. Then bursts into animation, hopping and smiling again. "Okay, I promise!" Her lips attacking me with kisses.

The others don't really seem surprised to see me alive. They don't really care.

We all get drunk again, hanging out in the dry section of Chili's, sending Spyder into the bloody swamp to retrieve bottles of whiskey and vodka.

Finally someone mentions the bat'leth inside of me.

"Can't you get it out?" Jen asks, cocking her bald head like a parrot in her white-feathered coat.

"I don't think so," I say.

She grabs onto a handle and tries to pull. No luck.

"It's stuck," she says.

Jen's eyes are losing color. A filmy haze over them. Like snakes before shedding their skin.

"You seem different," I say. "Have you broken out of your mold?"

"No," she says. "I'm still trying."

She still seems different. Not the same person at all. There's a lack of emotion in her. Her voice and movements are almost mechanical.

"I can do it, yo," Cedrik interrupts us, tugging on my bat'leth without warning.

It doesn't budge.

Brock comes over and takes his turn. He flexes his muscles

as hard as he can, but it doesn't come out. He tries again, this time with his shirt off, but that doesn't help.

"It's like the sword in the stone," Brock says. "Only the man who will be king can pull it out of you."

I get drunk far too easily. Probably from the lack of blood in my body. Everything appears in disarray.

We are running through the mall crazy again. The bat'leth cuts open my shirt, revealing my gory insides to everyone. They don't seem to mind. Red chunks of meat plop out of me, leaving a trail of guts for others to follow. Intestines roll out of me like spaghetti, tripping me when I run too fast.

Chloe throws me against a yo-yo cart to see if I will stick. The Bat'leth pierces through the wood, nailing me to the spot. I can't free myself. She tortures and molests my body as I drift in and out of consciousness.

I spend a few hours trying to get loose, watching the others and their activities. Spyder is not participating in craziness. He's back at the entrance, staring through the doors. He seems a little closer to the door than last time, but only by a few feet at most.

The walls seem to be changing colors and textures. They are cold and scaled, like a fish.

I think Jen is walking up the walls, naked and spider-like.

"I found it," Chloe says, appearing in front of me in black thong underwear, a garter belt, fishnet thigh-highs, a Dr. Seuss hat, and a chainsaw.

"I'll get you off of there lickety-split," she says with a big cartoon face.

CHAPTER EIGHT

I wake up alone in the Sears bedroom display, lying sideways. A square of wood attached to my back. My blankets are missing, but there's a heap of clothes on top of me, and boots, and french fries.

My insides are spilled out all over the sheets. I stand up and coil the dangling intestines around my left arm so I don't trip over them, leaving a pile of red gunk among the clothes.

I'm no longer wearing a shirt and my pants are all soggy with blood. I try to find something that fits from the clothes on the bed, but everything has this green fuzz on them. I go to the men's clothing section. These clothes have green fuzz on them as well. All the clothes in the store do. They haven't been vandalized by the crazed people, it's like some kind of mold. I'm scared to put them on. I don't want my wound infected. There's a pair of tennis shoes that don't look too bad, so I slip those on.

Out in the mall: Even more of a wasteland than ever, but now all the rubble and trash is beginning to grow moss and weeds. Some of the lights are flickering or broken.

I hear rain. Don't see it, but it's coming from the distance. I look out of the east entrance, it isn't raining outside. Though I do notice there aren't any people out there anymore. They must have all gone home. The parking lot is completely empty. No signs of life, or cars, for as far as I can see.

Jen is stuck to the wall, five feet off the ground between Just Sports and Hallmark. It's like she's been glued there. She's asleep, snoring gently, cuddling up against the wall as if it were the most normal place to sleep in the world.

I'm probably hallucinating.

Closer inspection: her waist is at eyelevel, she's wrapped in a blanket, her bald head pressed into a pillow. Just sleeping

78

there. On the wall. Like gravity has gotten confused.

I pull a corner of her blanket off of the wall and let go. Instead of drooping down toward the floor, it drops back to the wall. Exactly as if the wall has its own gravity.

Jen is sleeping snug and cozy up there, her mouth in a half-smile. I decide not to wake her. She might fall off the wall if I wake her.

I continue following the rain sound until I get to the Dillard's entrance. It is completely black inside of there and the sprinkler system is on, showering the darkness.

Somebody must have set the place on fire.

The water is slightly warm as I enter, drenching my guts and what's left of my hair. The place is completely charred. Absolutely nothing is recognizable. Just black coal on an ash-muddy ground. The second floor seems to have caved in. I can't maneuver very well. And the light from the entrance only illuminates a small portion of the store.

Walking back, I step into Brock. He is lying on a large lump of black coal which was probably a dresser or desk before the fire. I kick him. Dead. Definitely not killed by the fire, but perhaps smoke inhalation.

Rolling him over, I find gruesome wounds on his chest. He wasn't killed by smoke. He was murdered. Rubbing water out of my eyes—they look like chainsaw wounds.

"That bitch," I say to the charcoal, charging out of the remains of Dillard's.

Scampering through the trash and debris, holding my soggy guts and screaming Chloe's name. There are smashing sounds coming out of Game Stop, sparks and electronic pieces blasting out of the store. Spyder is in there with the sledgehammer, destroying all the Xboxes, Gamecubes, PS2s, and televisions.

He's cursing at everything he smashes, in words too snarled to identify. I call out to him, but he doesn't hear me. I have to throw a chunk of my guts at him, splatting against his shoulder, to get his attention.

"What the fuck are you doing?" he cries, the sledgehammer raised at me.

"Brock's dead," I say.

"I figured all of them were dead by now," Spyder says, disinterested. "After that explosion last night."

"He didn't die in the fire," I say. "He was murdered."

"Of course he was," Spyder says.

"Chloe did it."

"What?" He approaches me, very interested now. "How do you know?"

"She promised not to kill anyone else," I tell him. "After I survived, I didn't want anything to happen to her, I didn't think she—"

Spyder gets the general idea and walks out of the store, not saying a word.

I follow Spyder to the Food Court, where Chloe is eating a Big Mac on the only table standing. She smiles when she sees us, cheeks full of hamburger. Wearing a new black dress.

80

"You promised," I scream at her.

Spyder slams the sledgehammer into her food tray, making her jump back in her seat. The thud echoes through the junkland.

"What the hell?" Chloe cries.

Spyder boots her out of her chair and raises the sledgehammer over his head.

"Give me a reason not to," Spyder says.

"What's going on?" Chloe asks me.

"Why?" I ask her. "You promised. Why'd you have to kill Brock?"

She raises her arms in the air, spits pieces of Big Mac out of her mouth. "I didn't kill anyone!"

"Try lying one more time," Spyder says.

She stands, wipes food from her dress. "I am the killer. I admit it." She looks at me. "But, John, I swear to you. I didn't kill Brock. What happened to him?"

"I'm sorry," I say. "I just can't believe you."

"But you have to believe me. Look, there might be another killer. I only killed the cowboy and the Jesus freak. I didn't even kill the housewife or the old man. At first, I thought they must have just killed themselves. But it's possible somebody else killed them. And Brock."

Spyder and I look at each other. We're not sure what to believe.

"Let me see Brock's body," she says. "I don't care what you do to me, just give me a chance to prove that I didn't break my promise."

Spyder looks over her shoulder at me.

I nod.

Spyder drags Chloe by her hair all the way to Dillard's.

Entering the black shower, I lead us through to . . .

Something not human is here, perched over Brock's corpse. It has two pairs of long bony arms, gray checker-patterned skin, woman's breasts. I approach quietly.

It is Jen. She is naked in the rain, snake-stretching her body in a slow kind of dance. Something has happened to her. Something changed her. Slits open up on her hips and another pair of arms grow out of her sides, swaying with her motions.

She sees me. Turns her bald head at me, still the same face I saw when she was asleep on the wall, but now with black insect-like eyes and a mouthful of shark teeth.

"I did it," Jen says to us with a jagged smile, a pulsating voice. "I finally broke out of my mold."

I step back until I'm behind Spyder and his sledgehammer.

She turns away from us and lowers herself onto Brock's corpse. Her arms, now as long as legs, wrap around his sides and she lowers her crotch to his, as if getting ready to mate. Something shoots out of her cunt and rips into Brock's inner thigh. Some kind of mouth. Like a vaginal version of Giger's Alien mouth. It strikes out at the corpse and bites into him, retracting as quickly as it strikes.

Jen's body squirms and flexes in orgasm as the mouth snaps in and out of her, feeding on Brock's flesh. Her electrical moans echo in the charred room.

"Let's get out of here," Spyder says, slowly backing away to the exit.

We find Cedrik in the back of Musicland, curled in a ball, shivering.

"Lock the door," Spyder tells me.

I pull down the shutters and bolt the door, as Spyder makes sure Cedrik is okay. The kid's not speaking. Looks like he's on a bad trip.

Spyder goes back to Chloe, pushes her against the wall. "What's going on here? What the fuck did you do to her?"

"I didn't do anything," Chloe cries. "I don't know what's going on."

"She broke out of her mold, like you wanted," Spyder says.

"I didn't think she'd take it that literally." She giggles.

Spyder swings the sledgehammer at the wall next to her. She stops laughing. He notices she is shaking.

"You're saying you have nothing to do with any of this outside of the murders?" Spyder asks. "You don't know why we can't leave?"

She shakes her head.

"Bullshit!" Spyder shrieks.

I have to hold him back from her, making sure the bat'leth in my guts doesn't skewer him or Chloe.

"This is some kind of secret military experiment," Spyder says. "And you're in on it!"

Chloe shakes her head at him. "I just wanted you people to be more interesting."

"What, like you?" Spyder says. "You think you're not mundane?" He points at the kid on the ground. "You're like the Cedrik of the goth world."

"You don't know anything about me!" she cries. "If you did you'd know I'm not mundane, but you didn't even give me a chance!"

"Did you give the others a chance?" Spyder says. "Did you know every detail about them before condemning them to death?"

Chloe turns her head, tears in her eyes.

"Who do you work for?" Spyder asks her, raising the sledgehammer again. "I'm giving you one last chance."

Chloe is crying, black makeup running down her face.

"3 . . ." he counts down. "2 . . ."

"Spyder, don't," I grab for the hammer, but he pushes me

away. "She has nothing to do with this."

He's not listening to me. A dead stare at Chloe, mumbling some kind of chant to himself.

Cedrik screams, breaking our concentration.

Spyder goes to him.

"What's wrong?" he asks the kid.

Cedrik is drenched in sweat, grinding his teeth, rapid-breathing through his nose.

Spyder tries to help him to his feet, but he can't move him. His arms won't leave his lap.

"What the . . ." Spyder realizes his arms and legs are fused together, his chin melting into his knees.

"He's changing, too," I say.

Spyder tears off Cedrik's shirt to reveal a circuit board in his chest, meat tubes worming out of him.

"What the fuck!" Spyder screams, jumping away from him.

I notice something unusual on Cedrik's back.

"What's this?" I ask, getting a closer look.

His back has become a mall directory. A light underneath his skin illuminates the map.

"What are these?" Spyder asks, pointing to red dots on the map.

"That's us," I say. "In Musicland."

"Then what's this?" Spyder asks, pointing to a large red dot moving along the map toward our dots.

The creature that was Jen is at the entrance to Musicland, hooked onto the shutters like a giant insect made of human flesh, her breasts and crotch squished against the glass.

"All the mundanes must die," the creature says.

It chews through the shutters, then the door, and slithers into the room with us.

"Fucking bitch," Spyder says, raising the sledgehammer.

It leaps at Spyder, but he ducks out of the way, whipping his body around to attack. He swings the sledgehammer at her, but the creature dodges and the hammer slips out of his hands, flying across the room into Cedrik's head. The kid's skull explodes on impact. Blood and sparks spray across the pop music CDs.

I run to Chloe, who can't tear her eyes off of Jen's mutated body, almost aroused by her. Trying to snap her out of it, Spyder comes up from behind me and rips the bat'leth out of my back, taking my entire stomach with it.

Chloe drops her jaw at the hole in my stomach. She puts her arm all the way through me and wiggles her fingers on the other side.

Spyder cuts the creature in half with the Bat'leth. It falls over Cedrik's corpse, thrashing its limbs for a few minutes before going limp.

Chloe still has her arm inside of me. I push her out and approach the creature's remains.

Spyder looks at me and shakes his head. He drops the Klingon weapon, spits at Chloe, and leaves the store.

I follow him, trying to cover up the enormous hole in my torso so that nobody can look through me.

He goes downstairs to the east entrance. Without flinching, he opens the door and goes through. I watch him march across the deserted parking lot that stretches all the way into the horizon.

He doesn't look back.

Chloe steps up next to me, facing the door.

"Did he leave?" she asks.

"Walked right out," I say.

"So is it over?" she asks. "Can you leave?"

"The mall isn't menstruating anymore," I say. "But I still can't leave."

She holds my hand, looks out at the landscape of parking lot.

"You should leave," I tell her. "You're able to, why don't you just go?"

She looks at me, soft eyes.

"I don't want to."

"Maybe you can help me get out," I say. "You can go get help. Tie a rope to me and drag me out."

"I still like it here," she says.

She breathes in the wasteland of mall. "I want us to stay."

CHAPTER NINE

Days pass. We are beginning to break out of our molds. Chloe has grown large demon wings out of the demon wing tattoos on her back. Her eyes have turned into ball bearings. Her hair into porcupine quills. A devil's tail and webbed toes. Her canine teeth have extended into vampire fangs, just like she always wanted. And her paper white skin is slightly green-tinted and smooth like vinyl.

I become something less demonic, more stick-like and skeletal. The hole in my stomach widens and heals. The spinal column dissolves, replaced by two smaller cartilage poles running from my pelvis up my hips and chest, meeting at my chin. My legs become grasshopper-like. I'm able to leap up to the second floor of the mall very easily, or across the entire food court. I have also grown a tail, but it's not flesh. It is a cord, no different than a toaster's. My face remains human, but my hair falls out. And my skin changes into a moving picture: a blue sky full of billowy clouds slowly creeping across my flesh.

The mall changes as well. Plants and vegetation grow out of the rubble, creating a lush garden paradise. Strange hybrid animals are growing on trees in the 28 Days Later movie theater, dropping into the seats once ripened. There are tarantula/dogs, turtle/bunnies, lizard/ferrets roaming the mall and eating the orange-gray fruits that grow inside of Sears.

Chloe loves our new world, loves her new body and my body. She loves to fly around the mall, dancing and twisting through the air. I am mostly hollow now and light enough for her to carry, as she swoops down to pick me up. She licks the clouds on my face and fucks me in midair.

The mall's food supply runs out, so Chloe begins hunting the mutant animals in the mall, tearing into them with her vampire fangs. I discover that I don't need to eat. I just plug my tail into an outlet on the wall and feed off of the electricity. The power and water are never shut off in the mall for some reason. As if there's somebody out there keeping us alive.

Our offspring are born three at a time. They come out human but after half a dozen years they begin to break out of their molds and become something different. Each one a new and unique breed: the electric scorpion girl, the helicopter-faced boy, the girl with music playing out of her eyes.

Life is never what you expect it to be. You want it to be happy and peaceful. You want to get a good job, find a good wife, have kids, raise them just right, die without debts. But sometimes, for some people, chaos takes over and spoils the great plan. It pushes you in a direction you never thought you'd travel before, keeps you away from the life you truly wanted. But for these very unlucky people, despite their adversity and turmoil, usually turn out to be the most interesting. I, myself, a mirror of the society I left behind, have been unlucky enough to become interesting.

ABOUT THE AUTHOR

Carlton Mellick III is one of the leading authors of the bizarro fiction subgenre. Since 2001, his books have drawn an international cult following despite the fact that they have been shunned by most libraries and chain bookstores.

He won the Wonderland Book Award for his novel, *Warrior Wolf Women of the Wasteland*, in 2009. His short fiction has appeared in *Vice Magazine, The Year's Best Fantasy and Horror #16, The Magazine of Bizarro Fiction,* and *Zombies: Encounters with the Hungry Dead*, among others. He is also a graduate of Clarion West, where he studied under the likes of Chuck Palahniuk, Connie Willis, and Cory Doctorow.

He lives in Portland, OR, the bizarro fiction mecca.

Visit him online at **www.carltonmellick.com**

Bizarro books

CATALOG   SPRING 2011

Bizarro Books publishes under the following imprints:

www.rawdogscreamingpress.com

www.eraserheadpress.com

www.afterbirthbooks.com

www.swallowdownpress.com

For all your Bizarro needs visit:

WWW.BIZARROCENTRAL.COM

Introduce yourselves to the bizarro fiction genre and all of its authors with the Bizarro Starter Kit series. Each volume features short novels and short stories by ten of the leading bizarro authors, designed to give you a perfect sampling of the genre for only $10.

BB-0X1
"The Bizarro Starter Kit"
(Orange)

Featuring D. Harlan Wilson, Carlton Mellick III, Jeremy Robert Johnson, Kevin L Donihe, Gina Ranalli, Andre Duza, Vincent W. Sakowski, Steve Beard, John Edward Lawson, and Bruce Taylor.
236 pages $10

BB-0X2
"The Bizarro Starter Kit"
(Blue)

Featuring Ray Fracalossy, Jeremy C. Shipp, Jordan Krall, Mykle Hansen, Andersen Prunty, Eckhard Gerdes, Bradley Sands, Steve Aylett, Christian TeBordo, and Tony Rauch. **244 pages $10**

BB-0X2
"The Bizarro Starter Kit"
(Purple)

Featuring Russell Edson, Athena Villaverde, David Agranoff, Matthew Revert, Andrew Goldfarb, Jeff Burk, Garrett Cook, Kris Saknussemm, Cody Goodfellow, and Cameron Pierce **264 pages $10**

BB-001"The Kafka Effekt" D. Harlan Wilson - A collection of forty-four irreal short stories loosely written in the vein of Franz Kafka, with more than a pinch of William S. Burroughs sprinkled on top. **211 pages $14**

BB-002 "Satan Burger" Carlton Mellick III - The cult novel that put Carlton Mellick III on the map ... Six punks get jobs at a fast food restaurant owned by the devil in a city violently overpopulated by surreal alien cultures. **236 pages $14**

BB-003 "Some Things Are Better Left Unplugged" Vincent Sakwoski - Join The Man and his Nemesis, the obese tabby, for a nightmare roller coaster ride into this postmodern fantasy. **152 pages $10**

BB-004 "Shall We Gather At the Garden?" Kevin L Donihe - Donihe's Debut novel. Midgets take over the world, The Church of Lionel Richie vs. The Church of the Byrds, plant porn and more! **244 pages $14**

BB-005 "Razor Wire Pubic Hair" Carlton Mellick III - A genderless humandildo is purchased by a razor dominatrix and brought into her nightmarish world of bizarre sex and mutilation. **176 pages $11**

BB-006 "Stranger on the Loose" D. Harlan Wilson - The fiction of Wilson's 2nd collection is planted in the soil of normalcy, but what grows out of that soil is a dark, witty, otherworldly jungle... **228 pages $14**

BB-007 "The Baby Jesus Butt Plug" Carlton Mellick III - Using clones of the Baby Jesus for anal sex will be the hip sex fetish of the future. **92 pages $10**

BB-008 "Fishyfleshed" Carlton Mellick III - The world of the past is an illogical flatland lacking in dimension and color, a sick-scape of crispy squid people wandering the desert for no apparent reason. **260 pages $14**

BB-009 **"Dead Bitch Army" Andre Duza** - Step into a world filled with racist teenagers, cannibals, 100 warped Uncle Sams, automobiles with razor-sharp teeth, living graffiti, and a pissed-off zombie bitch out for revenge. **344 pages $16**

BB-010 **"The Menstruating Mall" Carlton Mellick III** - "The Breakfast Club meets Chopping Mall as directed by David Lynch." - Brian Keene **212 pages $12**

BB-011 **"Angel Dust Apocalypse" Jeremy Robert Johnson** - Meth-heads, man-made monsters, and murderous Neo-Nazis. "Seriously amazing short stories..." - Chuck Palahniuk, author of Fight Club **184 pages $11**

BB-012 **"Ocean of Lard" Kevin L Donihe / Carlton Mellick III** - A parody of those old Choose Your Own Adventure kid's books about some very odd pirates sailing on a sea made of animal fat. **176 pages $12**

BB-015 **"Foop!" Chris Genoa** - Strange happenings are going on at Dactyl, Inc, the world's first and only time travel tourism company. "A surreal pie in the face!" - Christopher Moore **300 pages $14**

BB-020 **"Punk Land" Carlton Mellick III** - In the punk version of Heaven, the anarchist utopia is threatened by corporate fascism and only Goblin, Mortician's sperm, and a blue-mohawked female assassin named Shark Girl can stop them. **284 pages $15**

BB-021**"Pseudo-City" D. Harlan Wilson** - Pseudo-City exposes what waits in the bathroom stall, under the manhole cover and in the corporate boardroom, all in a way that can only be described as mind-bogglingly irreal. **220 pages $16**

BB-023 **"Sex and Death In Television Town" Carlton Mellick III** - In the old west, a gang of hermaphrodite gunslingers take refuge from a demon plague in Telos: a town where its citizens have televisions instead of heads. **184 pages $12**

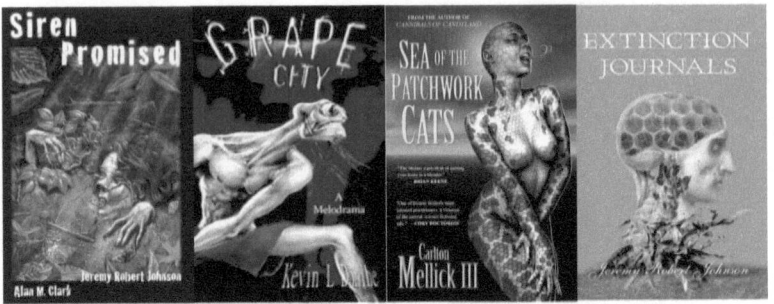

BB-027 "Siren Promised" Jeremy Robert Johnson & Alan M Clark
- Nominated for the Bram Stoker Award. A potent mix of bad drugs, bad dreams, brutal bad guys, and surreal/incredible art by Alan M. Clark. **190 pages $13**

BB-030 "Grape City" Kevin L. Donihe - More Donihe-style comedic bizarro about a demon named Charles who is forced to work a minimum wage job on Earth after Hell goes out of business. **108 pages $10**

BB-031"Sea of the Patchwork Cats" Carlton Mellick III - A quiet dreamlike tale set in the ashes of the human race. For Mellick enthusiasts who also adore The Twilight Zone. **112 pages $10**

BB-032 "Extinction Journals" Jeremy Robert Johnson - An uncanny voyage across a newly nuclear America where one man must confront the problems associated with loneliness, insane dieties, radiation, love, and an ever-evolving cockroach suit with a mind of its own. **104 pages $10**

BB-034 "The Greatest Fucking Moment in Sports" Kevin L. Donihe
- In the tradition of the surreal anti-sitcom Get A Life comes a tale of triumph and agape love from the master of comedic bizarro. **108 pages $10**

BB-035 "The Troublesome Amputee" John Edward Lawson - Disturbing verse from a man who truly believes nothing is sacred and intends to prove it. **104 pages $9**

BB-037 "The Haunted Vagina" Carlton Mellick III - It's difficult to love a woman whose vagina is a gateway to the world of the dead. **132 pages $10**

BB-042 "Teeth and Tongue Landscape" Carlton Mellick III - On a planet made out of meat, a socially-obsessive monophobic man tries to find his place amongst the strange creatures and communities that he comes across. **110 pages $10**

BB-043 "War Slut" Carlton Mellick III - Part "1984," part "Waiting for Godot," and part action horror video game adaptation of John Carpenter's "The Thing." **116 pages $10**

BB-045 "Dr. Identity" D. Harlan Wilson - Follow the Dystopian Duo on a killing spree of epic proportions through the irreal postcapitalist city of Bliptown where time ticks sideways, artificial Bug-Eyed Monsters punish citizens for consumer-capitalist lethargy, and ultraviolence is as essential as a daily multivitamin. **208 pages $15**

BB-047 "Sausagey Santa" Carlton Mellick III - A bizarro Christmas tale featuring Santa as a piratey mutant with a body made of sausages. 124 pages $10

BB-048 "Misadventures in a Thumbnail Universe" Vincent Sakowski - Dive deep into the surreal and satirical realms of neo-classical Blender Fiction, filled with television shoes and flesh-filled skies. **120 pages $10**

BB-049 "Vacation" Jeremy C. Shipp - Blueblood Bernard Johnson leaved his boring life behind to go on The Vacation, a year-long corporate sponsored odyssey. But instead of seeing the world, Bernard is captured by terrorists, becomes a key figure in secret drug wars, and, worse, doesn't once miss his secure American Dream. **160 pages $14**

BB-053 "Ballad of a Slow Poisoner" Andrew Goldfarb Millford Mutter-wurst sat down on a Tuesday to take his afternoon tea, and made the unpleasant discovery that his elbows were becoming flatter. **128 pages $10**

BB-055 "Help! A Bear is Eating Me" Mykle Hansen - The bizarro, heart-warming, magical tale of poor planning, hubris and severe blood loss...
150 pages $11

BB-056 "Piecemeal June" Jordan Krall - A man falls in love with a living sex doll, but with love comes danger when her creator comes after her with crab-squid assassins. **90 pages $9**

BB-058 "The Overwhelming Urge" Andersen Prunty - A collection of bizarro tales by Andersen Prunty. **150 pages $11**

BB-059 "Adolf in Wonderland" Carlton Mellick III - A dreamlike adventure that takes a young descendant of Adolf Hitler's design and sends him down the rabbit hole into a world of imperfection and disorder. **180 pages $11**

BB-061 "Ultra Fuckers" Carlton Mellick III - Absurdist suburban horror about a couple who enter an upper middle class gated community but can't find their way out. **108 pages $9**

BB-062 "House of Houses" Kevin L. Donihe - An odd man wants to marry his house. Unfortunately, all of the houses in the world collapse at the same time in the Great House Holocaust. Now he must travel to House Heaven to find his departed fiancee. **172 pages $11**

BB-064 "Squid Pulp Blues" Jordan Krall - In these three bizarro-noir novellas, the reader is thrown into a world of murderers, drugs made from squid parts, deformed gun-toting veterans, and a mischievous apocalyptic donkey. **204 pages $12**

BB-065 "Jack and Mr. Grin" Andersen Prunty - "When Mr. Grin calls you can hear a smile in his voice. Not a warm and friendly smile, but the kind that seizes your spine in fear. You don't need to pay your phone bill to hear it. That smile is in every line of Prunty's prose." - Tom Bradley. **208 pages $12**

BB-066 "Cybernetrix" Carlton Mellick III - What would you do if your normal everyday world was slowly mutating into the video game world from Tron? **212 pages $12**

BB-072 "Zerostrata" Andersen Prunty - Hansel Nothing lives in a tree house, suffers from memory loss, has a very eccentric family, and falls in love with a woman who runs naked through the woods every night. **144 pages $11**

BB-073 **"The Egg Man" Carlton Mellick III** - It is a world where humans reproduce like insects. Children are the property of corporations, and having an enormous ten-foot brain implanted into your skull is a grotesque sexual fetish. Mellick's industrial urban dystopia is one of his darkest and grittiest to date. **184 pages $11**

BB-074 **"Shark Hunting in Paradise Garden" Cameron Pierce** - A group of strange humanoid religious fanatics travel back in time to the Garden of Eden to discover it is invested with hundreds of giant flying maneating sharks. **150 pages $10**

BB-075 **"Apeshit" Carlton Mellick III** - Friday the 13th meets Visitor Q. Six hipster teens go to a cabin in the woods inhabited by a deformed killer. An incredibly fucked-up parody of B-horror movies with a bizarro slant. **192 pages $12**

BB-076 **"Fuckers of Everything on the Crazy Shitting Planet of the Vomit At smosphere" Mykle Hansen** - Three bizarro satires. Monster Cocks, Journey to the Center of Agnes Cuddlebottom, and Crazy Shitting Planet. **228 pages $12**

BB-077 **"The Kissing Bug" Daniel Scott Buck** - In the tradition of Roald Dahl, Tim Burton, and Edward Gorey, comes this bizarro anti-war children's story about a bohemian conenose kissing bug who falls in love with a human woman. **116 pages $10**

BB-078 **"MachoPoni" Lotus Rose** - It's My Little Pony... *Bizarro* style! A long time ago Poniworld was split in two. On one side of the Jagged Line is the Pastel Kingdom, a magical land of music, parties, and positivity. On the other side of the Jagged Line is Dark Kingdom inhabited by an army of undead ponies. **148 pages $11**

BB-079 **"The Faggiest Vampire" Carlton Mellick III** - A Roald Dahl-esque children's story about two faggy vampires who partake in a mustache competition to find out which one is truly the faggiest. **104 pages $10**

BB-080 **"Sky Tongues" Gina Ranalli** - The autobiography of Sky Tongues, the biracial hermaphrodite actress with tongues for fingers. Follow her strange life story as she rises from freak to fame. **204 pages $12**

BB-081 **"Washer Mouth" Kevin L. Donihe** - A washing machine becomes human and pursues his dream of meeting his favorite soap opera star. **244 pages $11**

BB-082 **"Shatnerquake" Jeff Burk** - All of the characters ever played by William Shatner are suddenly sucked into our world. Their mission: hunt down and destroy the real William Shatner. **100 pages $10**

BB-083 **"The Cannibals of Candyland" Carlton Mellick III** - There exists a race of cannibals that are made of candy. They live in an underground world made out of candy. One man has dedicated his life to killing them all. **170 pages $11**

BB-084 **"Slub Glub in the Weird World of the Weeping Willows"**
Andrew Goldfarb - The charming tale of a blue glob named Slub Glub who helps the weeping willows whose tears are flooding the earth. There are also hyenas, ghosts, and a voodoo priest **100 pages $10**

BB-085 **"Super Fetus" Adam Pepper** - Try to abort this fetus and he'll kick your ass! **104 pages $10**

BB-086 **"Fistful of Feet" Jordan Krall** - A bizarro tribute to spaghetti westerns, featuring Cthulhu-worshipping Indians, a woman with four feet, a crazed gunman who is obsessed with sucking on candy, Syphilis-ridden mutants, sexually transmitted tattoos, and a house devoted to the freakiest fetishes. **228 pages $12**

BB-087 **"Ass Goblins of Auschwitz" Cameron Pierce** - It's Monty Python meets Nazi exploitation in a surreal nightmare as can only be imagined by Bizarro author Cameron Pierce. **104 pages $10**

BB-088 **"Silent Weapons for Quiet Wars" Cody Goodfellow** - "This is high-end psychological surrealist horror meets bottom-feeding low-life crime in a techno-thrilling science fiction world full of Lovecraft and magic..." -John Skipp **212 pages $12**

BB-089 "Warrior Wolf Women of the Wasteland" Carlton Mellick III
Road Warrior Werewolves versus McDonaldland Mutants...post-apocalyptic fiction has never been quite like this. **316 pages $13**

BB-090 "Cursed" Jeremy C Shipp
- The story of a group of characters who believe they are cursed and attempt to figure out who cursed them and why. A tale of stylish absurdism and suspenseful horror. **218 pages $15**

BB-091 "Super Giant Monster Time" Jeff Burk
- A tribute to choose your own adventures and Godzilla movies. Will you escape the giant monsters that are rampaging the fuck out of your city and shit? Or will you join the mob of alien-controlled punk rockers causing chaos in the streets? What happens next depends on you. **188 pages $12**

BB-092 "Perfect Union" Cody Goodfellow
- "Cronenberg's THE FLY on a grand scale: human/insect gene-spliced body horror, where the human hive politics are as shocking as the gore." -John Skipp. **272 pages $13**

BB-093 "Sunset with a Beard" Carlton Mellick III
- 14 stories of surreal science fiction. **200 pages $12**

BB-094 "My Fake War" Andersen Prunty
- The absurd tale of an unlikely soldier forced to fight a war that, quite possibly, does not exist. It's Rambo meets Waiting for Godot in this subversive satire of American values and the scope of the human imagination. **128 pages $11**

BB-095 "Lost in Cat Brain Land" Cameron Pierce
- Sad stories from a surreal world. A fascist mustache, the ghost of Franz Kafka, a desert inside a dead cat. Primordial entities mourn the death of their child. The desperate serve tea to mysterious creatures. A hopeless romantic falls in love with a pterodactyl. And much more. **152 pages $11**

BB-096 "The Kobold Wizard's Dildo of Enlightenment +2" Carlton Mellick III
- A Dungeons and Dragons parody about a group of people who learn they are only made up characters in an AD&D campaign and must find a way to resist their nerdy teenaged players and retarded dungeon master in order to survive. 232 **pages $12**

BB-097 **"My Heart Said No, but the Camera Crew Said Yes!"** **Bradley Sands** - A collection of short stories that are crammed with the delightfully odd and the scurrilously silly. **140 pages $13**

BB-098 **"A Hundred Horrible Sorrows of Ogner Stump"** **Andrew Goldfarb** - Goldfarb's acclaimed comic series. A magical and weird journey into the horrors of everyday life. **164 pages $11**

BB-099 **"Pickled Apocalypse of Pancake Island"** **Cameron Pierce** A demented fairy tale about a pickle, a pancake, and the apocalypse. **102 pages $8**

BB-100 **"Slag Attack"** **Andersen Prunty** - Slag Attack features four visceral, noir stories about the living, crawling apocalypse.A slag is what survivors are calling the slug-like maggots raining from the sky, burrowing inside people, and hollowing out their flesh and their sanity. **148 pages $11**

BB-101 **"Slaughterhouse High"** **Robert Devereaux** - A place where schools are built with secret passageways, rebellious teens get zippers installed in their mouths and genitals, and once a year, on that special night, one couple is slaughtered and the bits of their bodies are kept as souvenirs. **304 pages $13**

BB-102 **"The Emerald Burrito of Oz"** **John Skipp & Marc Levinthal** OZ IS REAL! Magic is real! The gate is really in Kansas! And America is finally allowing Earth tourists to visit this weird-ass, mysterious land. But when Gene of Los Angeles heads off for summer vacation in the Emerald City, little does he know that a war is brewing...a war that could destroy both worlds. **280 pages $13**

BB-103 **"The Vegan Revolution... with Zombies"** **David Agranoff** When there's no more meat in hell, the vegans will walk the earth. **160 pages $11**

BB-104 **"The Flappy Parts"** **Kevin L Donihe** - Poems about bunnies, LSD, and police abuse. You know, things that matter. **132 pages $11**

BB-105 "Sorry I Ruined Your Orgy" Bradley Sands - Bizarro humorist Bradley Sands returns with one of the strangest, most hilarious collections of the year. **130 pages $11**

BB-106 "Mr. Magic Realism" Bruce Taylor - Like Golden Age science fiction comics written by Freud, *Mr. Magic Realism* is a strange, insightful adventure that spans the furthest reaches of the galaxy, exploring the hidden caverns in the hearts and minds of men, women, aliens, and biomechanical cats. **152 pages $11**

BB-107 "Zombies and Shit" Carlton Mellick III - "Battle Royale" meets "Return of the Living Dead." Mellick's bizarro tribute to the zombie genre. **308 pages $13**

BB-108 "The Cannibal's Guide to Ethical Living" Mykle Hansen - Over a five star French meal of fine wine, organic vegetables and human flesh, a lunatic delivers a witty, chilling, disturbingly sane argument in favor of eating the rich.. **184 pages $11**

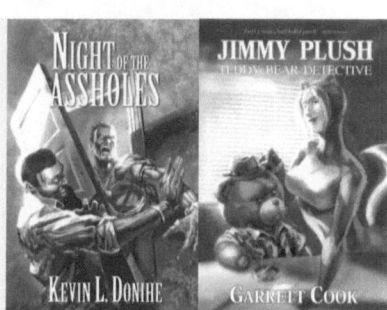

BB-109 "Starfish Girl" Athena Villaverde - In a post-apocalyptic underwater dome society, a girl with a starfish growing from her head and an assassin with sea anemone hair are on the run from a gang of mutant fish men. **160 pages $11**

BB-110 "Lick Your Neighbor" Chris Genoa - Mutant ninjas, a talking whale, kung fu masters, maniacal pilgrims, and an alcoholic clown populate Chris Genoa's surreal, darkly comical and unnerving reimagining of the first Thanksgiving. **303 pages $13**

BB-111 "Night of the Assholes" Kevin L. Donihe - A plague of assholes is infecting the countryside. Normal everyday people are transforming into jerks, snobs, dicks, and douchebags. And they all have only one purpose: to make your life a living hell.. **192 pages $11**

BB-112 "Jimmy Plush, Teddy Bear Detective" Garrett Cook - Hard-boiled cases of a private detective trapped within a teddy bear body. **180 pages $11**